纳西族三大史诗英译丛书

2016年国家社会科学基金项目成果（《纳西族东巴经主要典籍英译及研究》（项目批准号：16BYY034））

丛书主编　张立玉　起国庆

汉英对照

黑白之战

杨世光　整理　涂沙丽　英译
[美] H. W. Lan　审校

The War Between Dongzhu and Shuzhu

武汉大学出版社

图书在版编目(CIP)数据

黑白之战:汉英对照/杨世光整理;涂沙丽英译.—武汉:武汉大学出版社,2020.7
纳西族三大史诗英译丛书/张立玉,起国庆主编
　ISBN 978-7-307-21451-4

Ⅰ.黑… Ⅱ.①杨… ②涂… Ⅲ.纳西族—史诗—中国—汉、英 Ⅳ.I222.7

中国版本图书馆 CIP 数据核字(2020)第 060715 号

责任编辑:罗晓华　邓　喆　　责任校对:汪欣怡　　版式设计:韩闻锦

出版发行:武汉大学出版社　(430072　武昌　珞珈山)
　　　　　(电子邮箱:cbs22@whu.edu.cn　网址:www.wdp.com.cn)
印刷:武汉中远印务有限公司
开本:720×1000　1/16　　印张:14　　字数:164 千字
版次:2020 年 7 月第 1 版　　2020 年 7 月第 1 次印刷
ISBN 978-7-307-21451-4　　　　定价:40.00 元

版权所有,不得翻印;凡购我社的图书,如有质量问题,请与当地图书销售部门联系调换。

出品单位：中南民族大学南方少数民族文库翻译研究基地
云南省少数民族古籍整理出版规划办公室

纳西族三大史诗英译丛书
编委会

学术顾问　王宏印　李正栓

主　　编　张立玉　起国庆
副主编　李　明　和六花

编委会成员（按姓氏笔画排序）：
　　王向松　艾　芳　龙江莉　李克忠　李　明
　　杨筱奕　张立玉　和六花　依旺的　保俊萍
　　起国庆　陶开祥　涂沙丽　臧军娜

"三大史诗"前言

纳西族是滇西北地区的一个重要的少数民族，绝大部分居住在云南省丽江市，其余分布在云南其他县市和四川盐源、盐边、木里等县。作为较早创制本民族文字"东巴"文的民族之一，纳西族人民使用这一象形文字记录下了卷帙浩繁的东巴古籍文献，仅收藏于国内外有关学术文化机构和个人手中的东巴经文献就有近3万册，另有散佚于民间的东巴古籍更无法计数。

纳西族东巴经古籍分为祭天经、祭山神经、祭祖先经、求嗣经、祭猎神经、放替身经、解禳灾难经、祭水怪猛妖经、开丧经、祭死者经、祭风经、祭短鬼经、退口舌是非经、驱瘟神经、占卜经、道场规程经、零杂经等二十四类（参见和钟华、杨世光主编《纳西族文学史》，第81页，四川民族出版社，1992年），记载了大量的纳西族古典文学作品，包括神话故事、叙事长诗、天文地理、谚语歌谣等，较全面地反映了纳西族社会历史、文学艺术、哲学思想、宗教习俗、天文历法、民族关系等方面的内容，被誉为纳西族的"圣经"和纳西族古代社会的百科全书。

在数以万计的纳西东巴古籍中，最著名的纳西族神话史诗当属创世史诗《创世纪》、英雄史诗《黑白之战》（又名《东术战争》《董术战争》《东埃术埃》《董埃术埃》）和爱情史诗《鲁般鲁饶》，它们被合称为纳西族的三大史诗，又被誉为东巴文学中的"三颗明珠"。

《创世纪》记载于东巴经典籍祭山神龙王经、除秽经、祭风经、消灾经、开丧经、超荐经、求寿经、退口舌是非经等多部经书中，通过生动的神话故事和栩栩如生的人物形象观照出古代纳西族风俗礼仪起源、民族迁徙史、民族经济生活形态演进史，折射出纳西民族宇宙观、哲学观和审美观。《鲁般鲁饶》是一部纳西族叙事长诗，以东巴象形文字被记载于东巴古籍中，是纳西族殉情文学中最绚丽的诗篇。作为东巴经中一部重要的经书，《鲁般鲁饶》在大祭风仪式中必会被演诵。《黑白之战》是一部纳西族英雄史诗，被完整记载于纳西族东巴经籍中，根据东巴经书《东术战争》改编创作而成，直译是"东术仇斗"，即东部落与术部落的战争。《黑白之战》是丽江也是纳西族史上第一个国家艺术基金传播交流推广项目。

2008年3月1日，国务院颁布了首批《国家珍贵古籍名录》，110部少数民族文字古籍入选该名录，其中就包括了以《创世纪》和《东术战争》为代表的五部东巴经古籍，足见纳西族东巴史诗在少数民族古代文学体系中的重要地位。在新的社会历史条件下，对纳西族东巴经三大史诗展开英译工作，将有助于纳西族优秀传统文化在世界范围内的弘扬和传承。

2016年6月中南民族大学外语学院"英汉语言对比及应用研究团队"成功获批国家社会科学基金项目"纳西族东巴经主要典籍英译及研究"，致力于将纳西族东巴经三大史诗及其蕴涵的生态文化推向世界。项目团队在前期做了大量的文献学考证和民俗学调研的工作，在此基础上几易其稿，并聘请专家进行审校才最终完成《创世纪》《鲁般鲁饶》和《黑白之战》的英译定稿工作。

由于民族典籍多以诸如刻本、稿本、拓本、抄本的书写本形式或口耳相传的口头活态形式遗留下来，且一部典籍常常存在多个语种的版本，这就需要译者查找原始文献资料、搜集整理文献和进行版本考证，并借助文献注释进行翻译。在文献学考证阶段，团队成员充分利用学校图书馆、国家图书馆以及田野调查所在地丽江市的博物馆、研究院等机构，广泛搜集国内外有关三大史诗的文献资料，并对史诗的不同版本进行了系统梳理。

在审阅了诸多三大史诗的东巴文本和汉译版本后，团队最终确定以云南民族民间文学丽江调查队搜集、翻译、整理的《创世纪》(收录入2012年7月云南出版集团公司云南教育出版社出版的《云南少数民族叙事长诗全集》下卷)为《创世纪》英译本的汉语原文本。该版本系1958年9月由中共云南省委宣传部组织的云南民族民间文学丽江调查队在纳西族主要聚居地——丽江、宁蒗两地对纳西族文学进行发掘、整理和研究的成果。调查队将记载在经书中的《创世纪》翻译出了六个不同的底本，并根据在丽江和宁蒗搜集到的十余件口头流传材料和摩梭人口述材料，完成了《创世纪》的汉译整理工作。《鲁般鲁饶》英译本采用牛相奎、赵净修整理的《鲁般鲁饶》(收录入2012年7月云南出版集团公司云南教育出版社出版的《云南少数民族叙事长诗全集》中卷)为汉语原文本。该版本以由东巴经师和芳、和正才、多随合三人讲述，纳西族牛相奎、赵净修翻译的三种不同译文为主要依据，同时参考了周霖、和志武、和锡典等的三种译本，以及男女对唱形式的口头流传本《开美久命金和主本余冷排》《开美久命金和朱古羽勒排》和《东巴经·祭风部·本吕孔》等原始资料整理而成。《黑白之战》英译本采用杨世光根据东巴经典籍整理撰写的英雄史诗《东术战争》(收录于《云南少数民族古典史诗全集》上卷，于2009年9月由云南出版集团公司云南教育出版社出版）为汉语原文本。

由于民族典籍大多反映了各民族相异的语言、文学、传统、宗教以及价值观体系，因而译者只有经过充分的民俗学调研才能真正履行译者责任，不偏不倚地将原语典籍中承载的民族语言文化生态因子移植到译语生态环境中去。为此，团队成员多次前往云南省丽江市古城区、玉龙纳西族自治县等地开展田野调查，体验了"三朵节"、祭祖、婚礼庆典等一些具有浓郁纳西族特色的宗教民俗和传统节庆活动，并就纳西族民族起源和迁徙的相关历史传说，纳西族风俗礼仪、宗教意识与神灵观念，三大史诗在纳西族各方言区的流传等议题，对纳西族历史文化相关研究学者，如云南省社会科学院丽江东巴文化研究院相关领导及纳西学专家等，进行了深入访谈。

上述一系列文献学考证和民俗学调研工作给团队译者提供了大量关于纳西族东巴经典籍的原语生态信息，保证了译者对于原语生态环境的高度依归，为其后在文本移植过程中保留和再现纳西族生态因子打下了基础。

三大史诗英译本在翻译过程中得到了王宏印、李正栓等典籍英译学者的鼓励，得到了云南省少数民族古籍整理出版规划办公室主任起国庆、纳西族研究员和六花，以及丽江东巴文化研究院相关学者的指导和帮助，在此一并表示感谢。

译者团队几经润色，努力在内容表达和语体风格上再现神话史诗的原作风貌和纳西族的原语生态，但由于译者水平有限，加之原文仍有一些晦涩难解之处，译文处理不当在所难免，敬请广大读者朋友批评指正，以便修订时更正。

丛书主编：张立玉　起国庆

2020 年 1 月

前　言

　　《黑白之战》为纳西族英雄史诗，不仅是纳西族文学的巅峰之作，也堪称我国南方少数民族英雄史诗的典范之作，与创世史诗《创世纪》和爱情史诗《鲁般鲁饶》一同被誉为东巴文学中的"三颗明珠"。其汉译本较多，此次英译的原文采用的是由杨世光整理、汉译的《黑白之战》，由云南出版集团公司云南教育出版社于2009年出版发行。

　　这部史诗被完整记载于纳西族东巴经典籍中，纳西语原将其称为"东埃术埃"，意为东部落与术部落的战争。史诗围绕分住黑白两界的东族和术族的矛盾争斗展开。术主伺机偷东族的日月，东兵找回，术主启图再偷。之后，东主派机敏勇敢的阿璐王子巡守边界，致使术子米委无法得手。米委采用"调虎离山"计，但仍未得逞。最后，术主使出"美人计"，让女儿耿饶茨嫫去引诱阿璐王子。几番诱惑之下，阿璐王子终于陷入爱河，落入术主魔掌。阿璐宁死不屈，术主将其处死但仍一无所获。史诗结尾以东术决战，东族大获全胜而告终。史诗通过黑白两个部落争夺象征光明的日月的战争，传达了白界战胜黑界，光明战胜黑暗的鲜明主题，反映了纳西族人民的生命观念，以及自然崇拜、爱憎愿望、生活追求等朴素的哲理和思想。史诗结构严谨，矛盾集中，层次分明，情节紧凑，跌宕起伏，引人入胜。语言表达与艺术结构等方面也具有鲜明的纳西民族特色。

东巴古籍文献记载了纳西族千百年的辉煌文化，于2003年8月被联合国教科文组织列入世界记忆遗产名录。译者承担其中颇负盛名的英雄史诗《黑白之战》的翻译工作，深感责任之重大，若不用精益求精的精神来从事翻译及校对，既对不起读者，也对不起这样一部有价值的少数民族典籍。同时，这部典籍堪称纳西族古代社会的百科全书，涉及纳西民族宗教、历史、地理、风俗、生活文化及思考模式等诸多方面，译者深感翻译难度之大。为此，译者除了查阅大量相关文献之外，还多次到丽江进行实地考察，积极与纳西族文化研究专家沟通，并邀请在英汉文化比较领域从事多年研究的威斯康星州立大学的蓝海霞教授进行全书的审定，希望尽量将文化误读与误译降到最低限度，力图使译文忠实原文，并传神达意。

　　限于译者水平有限，疏漏或翻译不妥之处在所难免，恳请广大读者批评指正。

译者：涂沙丽

2019年9月

目　　录

第一章	天地始初	2
第二章	争战起源	8
第三章	术主行盗	14
第四章	日月重归	22
第五章	术子用计	30
第六章	米委丧生	42
第七章	乌鸦挑唆	50
第八章	术主寻衅	60
第九章	遣兵侦察	68
第十章	初战白海	80
第十一章	耿饶茨嫫	88
第十二章	阿璐上钩	100
第十三章	陷身魔窟	114
第十四章	术兵犯境	128
第十五章	宁死不屈	140
第十六章	茨嫫忏悔	154
第十七章	东主返世	164
第十八章	祖孙相逢	172
第十九章	东术决战	180
第二十章	光明永存	200

黑白之战

The War Between Dongzhu and Shuzhu

Contents

Chapter 1	The Beginning of Heaven and Earth	3
Chapter 2	The Cause of the War	9
Chapter 3	Shuzhu the Thief Lord	15
Chapter 4	The Sun and Moon Returned	23
Chapter 5	Shuzhu's Son's Trick	31
Chapter 6	The Death of Miwei	43
Chapter 7	The Meddling Crow	51
Chapter 8	Shuzhu's Provocation	61
Chapter 9	Scouts Dispatched	69
Chapter 10	First Battle at the White Sea	81
Chapter 11	Gengrao Cimo	89
Chapter 12	The Bait Swallowed	101
Chapter 13	Trapped	115
Chapter 14	Shu's Invasion	129
Chapter 15	Death over Betrayal	141
Chapter 16	Cimo's Confession	155
Chapter 17	Dongzhu's Return	165
Chapter 18	Family Reunion	173
Chapter 19	The Final Battle	181
Chapter 20	The Eternal Light	201

第一章　天地始初

千古万古前，
没有地和天，
没有日月星，
没有海和山。

妙音出上方，
瑞气出下方；
音和气相合，
刮起白风来。

三股白风吹，
化为白云彩；
白云酿露浆，
白露凝白蛋。

白蛋孵开来，
五神①出世来，

---

① 五神：五神分别为盘、禅、高、吾、恒。

Chapter 1　The Beginning of Heaven and Earth

Long long ago,
There was neither heaven nor earth,
Neither the sun, the moon, nor the stars,
Neither the seas nor the mountains.

The celestial melody descended from above,
And the auspicious vapor rose from below.
When the melody met the vapor,
The white wind began to blow.

Three gusts of the white wind
turned into white clouds.
Then the white clouds became white nectar,
Which congealed to form a white egg.

The white egg hatched,
From which came five deities①.

---

① Five deities: the five deities are called Pan, Chan, Gao, Wu and Heng, who were responsible for the five directions — the East, the South, the West, the North, and the Center.

黑白之战　The War Between Dongzhu and Shuzhu

东主①出世来，
术主②出世来。

有了白天地，
有了白山川，
有了白风雨，
有了白牛羊。

有了黑天地，
有了黑山川，
有了黑风雨，
有了黑牛羊。

有了红天地，
有了红山川，
有了红风雨，
有了红牛羊；

有了黄天地，
有了黄山川，
有了黄风雨，
有了黄牛羊；

---

① 东主：善神米利东主。
② 术主：黑界米利术主。

Along with them,
Came out Dongzhu① and Shuzhu.②

There appeared
White heaven and earth,
White mountains and rivers,
White wind and rain,
And white cattle and sheep.

There appeared
Black heaven and earth,
Black mountains and rivers,
Black wind and rain,
And black cattle and sheep.

There appeared
Red heaven and earth,
Red mountains and rivers,
Red wind and rain,
And red cattle and sheep.

There appeared
Yellow heaven and earth,
Yellow mountains and rivers,
Yellow wind and rain,
And yellow cattle and sheep.

---

① Dongzhu: the good deity Mili Dongzhu.
② Shuzhu: the wicked deity Mili Shuzhu.

有了绿天地，
有了绿山川，
有了绿风雨，
有了绿牛羊。

居那若倮山，
神山撑天地；
赠争含鲁石，①
神石镇妖孽。

三朵白云彩，
再酿白露浆；
白露有一滴，
化为达吉海。

山有山生物，
海有海生物，
万类在繁衍，
万物在繁昌。

---

① 赠争含鲁石：纳西语音译，即最早出现的石头。

Chapter 1 The Beginning of Heaven and Earth

There appeared
Green heaven and earth,
Green mountains and rivers,
Green wind and rain,
And green cattle and sheep.

Juna Ruoluo is the celestial mountain,
Which sustained heaven and earth.
Zengzheng Hanlu is the celestial rock, ①
Which could outdo all devils.

The three white clouds
Made more white nectar,
A drop of which
Became the Daji Sea.

All species,
On the mountains and in the seas,
Began to thrive
And to multiply.

---

① Zengzheng Hanlu: transliterated from the Naxi language, meaning the very first rock.

第二章　争战起源

米丽达吉海，
海宽连云天。
海水如玉液，
海浪似金毯。

海心长神树，
幼苗细又软。
像根头发辫，
来回飘浪间。

恶鬼要砍树，
天神不许砍；
天神吼一声，
恶鬼吓破胆。

术主要伤苗，
东主来阻挡；
斯族要伤苗，
哈族来防护。

Chapter 2 The Cause of the War

The Mili Daji Sea was
So vast that its edges seemed to touch the sky;
So clear that its waters looked like liquid jade;
So buoyant that its waves surged ahead like a golden carpet.

At its center was a celestial tree,
A little seedling slender and soft,
Like a hair braid
Surging with each wave.

The devil wanted to chop it down,
But Heaven would not allow it.
Heaven gave out a roar of displeasure,
And the devil was scared to death.

Shuzhu attempted to destroy the seedling,
Dongzhu came to defend it;
The Si people attempted to hurt the seedling,
The Ha people came to protect it.

恶鬼半夜来，
约着术族来，
约着斯族来，
偷偷把树砍。

天神领东族，
天神带哈族，
点下如意药，
断口重接好。

一天长三次，
一夜粗三次，
含英宝达树，
长成摩天树。

树分十二枝，
长出十二属；
枝生十二叶，
分出十二月。

叶是绸缎叶，
花是金银花；
珍珠结成串，
宝果压枝丫。

见了金银花，
见了珠宝果，
术与东争夺，
从此兴干戈。

The devil came at midnight
With Shu people,
With some Si people,
Together they stealthily cut the tree down.

The Dong and Ha people
Led by Heaven,
Applied the elixir
And revived the tree.

Growing three times taller each day,
And three times thicker each night,
The tree called Hanying Baoda
Was touching the sky.

Twelve branches grew out of the tree,
Each one of the earthly branches.
Twelve leaves sprouted from the branches,
Each a calendar month.

The leaves were of silk and satin,
And the flowers, of gold and silver.
Clusters of pearls,
The treasure fruits, weighing on the branches.

On seeing the gold and silver flowers
And the pearly fruits,
Shu and Dong began to fight for them,
The fight that has been going on ever since.

大拉久主海,
海在若倮山;
碧玉铺成浪,
黄金砌作岸。

一对金鲤鱼,
摆尾游起来。
吸水又吐水,
含着金蛋玩。

看鱼嘴开合,
饮水有了谱;
看鱼吞金蛋,
吃饭有了谱。

鱼要活命水,
人要吃穿戴;
术与东争抢,
从此动刀剑。

只待火星闪,
干柴就要燃;
只等引线动,
弩弓就要开。

平安人世间,
战云纷纷翻;
角与角相抵,
蹄与蹄相踩。

Chapter 2 The Cause of the War

Near the Ruoluo Mountain was
The Dala Jiuzhu Sea,
With waves of jade
And beaches of gold.

A pair of golden carps
Were swimming with their tails swaying.
Sipping and spitting the water,
They played with the gold egg with their mouths.

Their sipping and spitting
Became how we drink water.
Their catching and swallowing the gold egg
Became how we eat our meals.

As the fish depend on water,
We need food and clothing.
For these needs, Shuzhu and Dongzhu
Turned to blades and swords.

Like bundles of dry firewood,
They needed only a spark to burn;
Like a crossbow,
They needed only a pull to open.

The peace of the world
Was now shrouded in the warring clouds.
Horns locked with horns,
Hoofs trampling upon hoofs.

第三章　术主行盗

若倮神山高，
耸入九重天。
太阳从左旋，
月亮往右转。

绕行三十天，
相见在山顶。
一月三十天，
古谱在这里。

神山分两半，
神山有两界。
界东日月明，
界西似夜晚。

神裔米利东，
住在山东面。
九座白石屋，
白得像银墙。

Chapter 3　　Shuzhu the Thief Lord

Ruoluo the celestial mountain was high,
Reaching into the sky.
The sun orbited by from its left,
And the moon, its right.

After having traveled for thirty rounds,
They would meet at the mountain top.
The thirty days in a month
Originated from here.

The celestial mountain had two parts:
East and west.
East was bright with the sun and the moon,
While west was dark as night.

Dongzhu, the descendant of light,
Dwelled in the east
In nine white-stone houses,
As white as the silver-wall.

黑白之战
The War Between Dongzhu and Shuzhu

脚踏白的地,
头顶白的天。
太阳明晃晃,
月亮亮闪闪。

黑魔米利术,
住在山西面。
九座黑石屋,
黑得像焦炭。

脚踩黑的地,
头戴黑的天。
黑风呜呜吼,
黑云浑茫茫。

尖峰隔两界,
树木不相缠;
黑白截然分,
飞鸟不往来。

东主有银鼠,
打洞日夜忙。
埋头方向偏,
打穿若倮山。

洞口连白界,
洞尾通黑界。
金光漏出去,
银光漏出去。

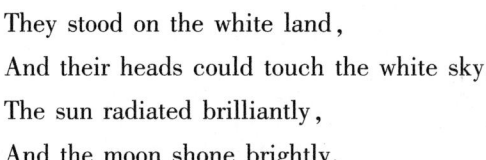

Chapter 3　Shuzhu the Thief Lord

They stood on the white land,
And their heads could touch the white sky.
The sun radiated brilliantly,
And the moon shone brightly.

Shuzhu, the descendant of darkness,
Lived in the west
In nine black-stone houses,
As black as the charcoal.

He stood on the dark land
And was crowned with the dark sky.
Sinister gales were constantly roaring,
And murky clouds were always rolling.

The mountain peak was the divide between the two,
And so their trees had nothing to do with each other.
Black and white were distinct from each other,
And their birds never visited each other.

Dongzhu had a silver rat,
Which burrowed day and night.
Straying from its path,
It dug its way through the Ruoluo mountain.

The tunnel started with the white world
And ended with the black one.
The golden light slipped out,
And the silver light was leaked out.

黑白之战
The War Between Dongzhu and Shuzhu

金光有一束，
照亮术的山；
银光有一道，
照进术的房。

术主见金光，
睁眼像铜钵；
术主见银光，
张口不会合。

东地有太阳，
术主早垂涎；
东地悬月亮，
术心冒醋酸。

要把光明掳，
忙叫黑猪来：
洞子再拱大，
洞口再拱宽。

挑水想搬井，
偷柴想背山。
贪口不解馋，
术主怀鬼胎。

Chapter 3 Shuzhu the Thief Lord

A ray of the golden light
Lit up Shuzhu's mountain.
A ray of the silvery light
Shone into Shuzhu's room.

Shuzhu, at the sight of the golden light,
Opened his eyes wide as a brass bowl.
On seeing the silvery light,
He opened his mouth too big to shut again.

Dongzhu had the sun,
Which Shuzhu had coveted for long.
Dongzhu had the moon,
Of which Shuzhu was envious.

To make the light his captive,
Shuzhu ordered the black hog
To shove the tunnel bigger,
To shove the tunnel wider.

Fetching well-water, he would take the well with him.
And stealing firewood from the mountain, he would carry the mountain back with him.
The greedy Shuzhu had not had enough,
So he hatched a plot.

遣贼去东界，
偷下金太阳，
窃下银月亮，
钻洞往回搬。

黑铁打铁链，
粗链拴太阳；
拴在铁柱上，
铁柱迸火光。

黑铜打铜链，
粗链拴月亮；
拴在铜柱上，
铜柱凝白霜。

He sent off a thief to the east

To steal the golden sun,

To steal the silvery moon,

And to move both back through the tunnel.

With the iron chain forged with black iron,

The sun was bound

And tied to an iron pillar,

Which gave off fiery sparks.

With the copper chain forged with black copper,

The moon was bound

And tied to a copper post,

Which then was covered with white frost.

第四章　日月重归

太阳丢失了，
月亮遗落了，
光明不见了，
东主发慌了。

抬头望术界，
白光冲上天。
猜是术主偷，
想是术家抬。

池里黄金蛙，
胆大如猛象，
心细如猎犬，
派去当侦探。

银鼠错打洞，
一日悔三回。
听蛙要出行，
找东来求情：

Chapter 4　The Sun and Moon Returned

The sun was missing;
The moon was lost;
The light was gone;
Dongzhu was panicking.

Seeing the bright light
On the other side,
He knew something was not quite right:
Shuzhu must have stolen the light.

The golden frog in the pond,
Brave as a raging elephant
And detailed as a hound,
Was sent to search as a scout.

That silver rat who misdug the hole
Repented for it three times a day.
On hearing that the frog was setting off,
He pleaded with Dongzhu.

"愿做金蛙伴,
愿去当侦探。
赎过要立功,
敢去踏火焰。"

金蛙和银鼠,
边走边商量。
半夜鸡叫前,
来到术地方。

术主做好梦,
鼾声呼呼响。
三绺黑头发,
沿床垂下来。

银鼠银牙尖,
好像一把剪。
上去咬头发,
三绺齐咬断。

清早术起床,
舀水来洗脸。
梳头头发断,
气得手打颤。

黑鼠蹲柱旁,
鼠牙像针尖。
术猜是它咬,
怒火烧牙关。

Chapter 4　The Sun and Moon Returned

"I would like to accompany the frog,
To be a scout.
To redeem my mistake with good deed,
I would risk my life."

Setting off, the golden frog and the sliver rat
Planned on the way.
They got to Shu's side when it was dark
Before the crowing of the rooster.

Shuzhu was fast asleep,
With thunderous snoring.
Three strands of his black hair
Hanging down from the bed.

The silver rat had sharp teeth,
As sharp as scissors.
It went up and chewed on the hair,
And cut off all three strands.

Shuzhu got up in the morning,
And fetched water to wash his face.
Combing his hair, he found it was cut,
And his hands shook with anger.

Seeing a black rat by the pillar
With its teeth sharp as needles,
Shuzhu thought it had cut his hair,
Grinding his teeth in anger.

拣根粗棍子,
掐住鼠脖子,
打翻在地上,
踩扁在地上。

蠢汉做蠢事,
铁柱无人守。
金蛙和银鼠,
偷偷笑不休。

金蛙去巡风,
银鼠奔上前。
咬断粗铁索,
放开金太阳。

金蛙守窗户,
银鼠奔铜柱。
咬断粗铜链,
放开银月亮。

银鼠扛月亮,
金蛙驮太阳,
嘻嘻哈哈笑,
赶回东地来。

东手挂月亮,
东掌托太阳,
秘咒念三遭,
谁也偷不了。

Chapter 4 The Sun and Moon Returned

He grabbed a thick stick,
Seized the rat by the throat,
Beat it down to the ground,
And stamped on it and flattened it.

Stupid is as stupid does,
So the pillar was unguarded.
The golden frog and the silver rat
Couldn't stop laughing in secret.

As the golden frog patrolled outside,
The silver rat went up,
Gnawed through the thick iron chain,
And freed up the golden sun.

With the golden frog guarding the window,
The silver rat rushed to the copper post.
It bit through the thick copper chain,
And freed up the silver moon.

With the moon on the rat's shoulder
And the sun on the frog's back,
To the east side they went back,
Full of joy and laughter.

Dongzhu hung up the moon with his hand
And held up the sun with his palm.
He then uttered a secret spell three times
To ensure it could not be stolen anymore.

黑白之战　The War Between Dongzhu and Shuzhu

黑暗还术地，
术界黑漆漆；
光明回东境，
东地亮晶晶。

Darkness returned to Shu's land,
Which was now pitch-black.
Light returned to Dong's land,
Which was now sparkling bright.

第四章 日月重归
Chapter 4 The Sun and Moon Returned

第五章　术子用计

米利东主啊，
爱儿有九个；
茨爪金嫫啊，
爱女有九个。

巴掌分五指，
不会一般齐；
九男和九女，
巧拙两分明。

美男名阿璐，
直树无疙瘩。
好像沙里金，
好像草里花。

好汉是阿璐，
能手夺天巧。
金嫫惜如珠，
东主爱如宝。

Chapter 5 Shuzhu's Son's Trick

Mili Dongzhu
Had nine sons;
Cizhua Jinmo
Had nine daughters.

The five fingers of the same hand
Cannot be the same.
The nine sons and daughters
Differed in their natural abilities.

The handsome son named Alu
Was as straight as a towering tree.
He was like the gold in the sand
Or a flower among the grass.

A good fellow was Alu,
Who was very capable.
Jinmo treasured him like a pearl,
And Dong loved him like a treasure.

骏马蹄生风,
早日架鞍子。
阿璐肩膀铁,
早日挑担子。

日月丢复得,
东主倍提防。
千斤交阿璐,
派去巡界边。

光明得又丢,
术主不甘心。
眉头皱成沟,
想起小儿子。

"安森米委呀,
心有七个窍,
像笛有七眼,
可吹百个调。

"好儿米委呀,
肠有九道弯,
像绳绕九曲,
捆宝靠你来!"

撵鹿狗有意,
遇狗鹿无心。
米委和阿璐,
碰头在边境。

Chapter 5 Shuzhu's Son's Trick

A magnificent steed that runs like wind
Is saddled earlier than others.
Alu with broad shoulders
Carried heavy loads earlier than others.

Since the loss and recovery of the sun and the moon
Dongzhu was doubly on guard.
He decided to send Alu
To patrol the borders.

Losing the stolen light,
Shuzhu would not accept his defeat.
Frowning fiercely,
He thought of his youngest son.

"Ansen Miwei
Was full of wicked ideas;
Like a flute with seven holes,
He could play hundreds of tunes.

"My dear son Miwei!
You are so smart
And ingenious
That I am counting on you to get them back!"

Like a deer and a dog,
An unaware deer and a hunting dog,
Miwei and Alu
Met at the border.

米委拉阿璐,
铺下白披毡。
掏出白骰子,
两人掷起来。

渔人下鱼饵,
诱鱼上钩来。
米委故意输,
阿璐花了眼。

米委笑着问:
"东天多光彩,
东地万物长,
是谁造出来?"

阿璐夸海口:
"天地日月星,
山川木石水,
都是我造的。"

鱼儿要上钩,
米委把饵添。
亲热像兄弟,
话里拌蜜糖:

"阿璐真能干,
阿璐赛神仙。
请来辟术地,
请来开术天。

Chapter 5 Shuzhu's Son's Trick

Miwei talked Alu into
Sitting down on a white felt rug.
He took out a white dice,
And the two started a game.

Like a fisherman who set the bait
To entice the fish,
Miwei lost the game on purpose,
While Alu was thrown even more off guard.

Grinning, Miwei asked,
"The east world has a sky so bright
And a land so fertile.
Who created it?"

Alu replied boastfully,
"The sun and the moon,
Mountains, rivers, forests, and waters,
They are all my work."

Seeing the fish was about to bite,
Miwei added more bait.
He spoke like the best of a brother
With honey-sweet words:

"Alu, you are as capable
As the immortal creators!
Please come to cultivate the Shu's land
And create a new Shu world!

"金银随你拿,
拿去用牛驮;
珠宝随你装,
装来用马驮。"

小鱼吞香饵,
不知钩刺藏:
"米委你放心,
隔天我就来。"

阿璐见父亲,
说要去术地。
东主忙摇头,
苦劝不让行:

"上山不提防,
魔鬼会来缠;
走路不小心,
脚会撞石块。

"狐狸不小心,
也会被虎咬;
男儿不听话,
会被仇人杀。"

阿璐见母亲,
说要去术地。
金嫫摆摆手,
拦住不准走:

"Take as much gold and silver
As your cattle allow you to carry;
Sack as many pearls and gems
As the horseback can bear."

The small fish bit the bait,
Unaware of the hidden hook:
"Miwei, don't you worry.
I will come in a couple of days."

When Alu told his father
That he would go to the west,
Dongzhu shook his head immediately,
Insisting that he not go:

"On the way up the mountains,
The devils haunt the unaware;
On the way to the west,
The rocks smash the feet of the careless.

"Even a fox, when careless of its environs,
Could be mauled by tigers;
Even a strong young man, if heedless of warnings,
Could suffer revenge."

Then Alu went to see his mother
About going to the west.
Jinmo waved her hands from side to side,
Blocking his way:

"三道鬼旋涡，
旋在你头上；
一道凶花纹，
刻在你手上。

"三个短命记，
烙在你腰间。
你要去仇家，
我心真不安。"

父亲劝九遍，
阿璐不点头；
母亲劝七遍，
阿璐光摇头：

"吃肉不兴吐，
说话不兴悔。
盟约订在先，
不去丢脸皮。"

妈啊没办法，
嘱儿莫大意；
爹呵劝不转，
授儿安身计：

"神鬼不一样，
东术不一般。
术地要斜辟，
术天要歪开。

"It is like having three devilish cowlicks
On your head;
And an ominous pattern
On your palm.

"It is like having three premature death marks
Seared around your waist.
You are going to our nemesis,
I feel very uneasy about it."

His father tried numerous times,
But Alu would not change his mind;
His mother tried repeatedly,
But Alu only shook his head:

"Eating the meat,
We are not supposed to spit it.
Going back on my words,
I would dishonor myself."

Out of other means,
His mother told him to be careful;
Persuading him in vain,
His father showed him how to protect himself:

"Deities and ghosts are different;
Dong's land and Shu's land differ.
Deal Shu's land and sky
With slanted strikes.

黑白之战　The War Between Dongzhu and Shuzhu

"黑白不一样，
东术非睦邦。
术山要斜辟，
术川要歪开。

"夜深狗不吠，
快回交界边。
栽起铜棘来，
安起铁铡来！"

"Black and white differ.
We have never been good neighbors.
Render Shu's mountains and streams
With angled blows.

"In the deepest night when dogs bark not,
Hurry back to the border.
Plant copper thorns,
And set up iron cutters!"

第六章　米委丧生

阿璐到术家，
米委笑脸迎。
阿璐显身手，
米委献殷勤。

挥斧开术天，
开得歪歪的，
好像草锅盖，
歪盖在云里。

舞剑劈术地，
劈成斜斜的，
好像木楼梯，
斜架在屋顶。

术王赠金银，
翠玉盘子装；
米委送珠宝，
五色丝线拴。

Chapter 6   The Death of Miwei

Alu arrived at Shu's land,
And Miwei greeted him with sugary smiles.
Pleased by Miwei's flattery,
Alu displayed his talent.

Swinging his axe,
Alu opened up the sky crookedly,
As a straw lid on a pan
Covering askew in the cloud.

Waving his sword,
He split the land tilted,
Like a wooden staircase
Propped up slantingly on the roof of a house.

Shuzhu presented him with gold and silver
On the plates of jade green;
Miwei gave him pearls and jewels
Strung up with colorful silk yarn.

黑白之战　The War Between Dongzhu and Shuzhu

蒙住阿璐心，
迷了阿璐眼，
爹妈临行话，
忘在耳后边。

一睡合眼皮，
鼾声如雷鸣。
米委暗暗笑，
忙去偷光明。

半夜人声静，
有狗也不吠。
心宽忘百忧，
沉睡如酒醉。

梦见恶狗扑，
猛然被惊醒。
财宝揣三把，
如风溜回程。

米委过界东，
上前盗日月；
阿璐落界西，
在后设陷阱。

东家穿山眼，
看见黑影闪。
黑手摘月亮，
月光乱摇晃。

Chapter 6　The Death of Miwei

Smitten
And charmed,
Alu had all forgotten
His parents' warnings.

He fell asleep fast
With thunderous snores at last.
Pleased with himself,
Miwei hurriedly went to steal the light.

In the quiet of the midnight,
Dogs didn't bark.
Content with no worries,
He slept like a drunkard.

Dreaming of a vicious dog attacking him,
He suddenly woke up.
Grabbing three handfuls of treasures,
He slipped homeward like wind.

Miwei already crossed the border,
And was about to steal the sun and the moon.
When Alu arrived at the border,
He set up his trap and waited.

Dongzhu could see through the mountains,
So he saw the dark shadow,
The dark hand picking the moon,
With the moon light shifting erratically.

黑白之战
The War Between Dongzhu and Shuzhu

东家顺风耳，
听见黑脚踩。
黑手扯太阳，
发出叮当响。

雷霆一声喊，
东兵追过来；
大风一声吼，
东将赶过来。

米委心发麻，
脚抖如跳蚤。
丢下日和月，
拼命往回逃。

铜棘勾双脚，
扑地嘴啃泥；
铁锏咔嚓响，
转眼命归阴。

千人围过来，
千声骂盗贼；
万人涌上来，
万嘴吐口水。

割下魔贼头，
来祭日月神。
血水洗刀刃，
界边来示警。

Chapter 6 The Death of Miwei

Dongzhu could hear from afar,
So he heard the dark feet treading.
The dark hand pulled on the sun
With jingling noises.

He shouted as the thunderbolt,
And his soldiers started the chasing;
He roared as the withering wind,
And his generals came over to him.

Miwei stood aghast,
Shivering like a flea.
He dropped the sun and the moon,
Running desperately for his life.

With his feet hooked by the copper thorns,
He fell on his face;
With the sound of the cutter,
He was instantly killed.

Thousands of people stepped forward,
Railing at the thief;
Tens and thousands gathered round,
Spitting on his face.

His devilish head was cut off
To make sacrifice to the sun and the moon.
His blood was used to wash the blade
To deter any more aggression at the border.

黑白之战　The War Between Dongzhu and Shuzhu

撬开九层土，
压着黑魔尸，
土上开水渠，
不让鬼翻身。

Digging up nice layers of dirt
To put on top of the black devilish corpse
And building a canal on top of the dirt,
They made sure his ghost would never return.

第七章　乌鸦挑唆

九层白土上，
开凿白水渠。
金锄遍地挥，
银锄漫天舞。

东家狗獾子，
挖沟多卖力；
东家吸风鹰，
扒土不愿歇。

乌鸦贪游玩，
跳来又跳去，
怕苦怕沾灰，
不扒一把土。

哪里有火烟，
它往哪里瞧；
哪里有血肉，
它朝哪里跑。

Chapter 7   The Meddling Crow

On top of the nine layers of white soil,
The canal-building was in full swing.
Gold hoes were plowing everywhere,
and silver pickaxes, swung in the air.

Dong's dog spared no efforts
In its digging;
The hawk took no breaks
In its hoeing.

But the crow larked about,
Jumping from branch to branch.
To avoid dirt and toil,
It touched no soil.

Wherever there were fire and smoke,
There was the crow looking around;
Wherever there were flesh and blood,
There was the crow running towards them.

黑白之战　The War Between Dongzhu and Shuzhu

毒刺生倒钩，
恶狗先咬人。
东主来沟边，
乌鸦挑是非：

"老鹰不开沟，
光朝火烟飞；
狗獾不扒土，
只往红肉奔。

"日出又日落，
挖土我最苦。
泥巴洗不净，
腰弯像张弓。"

乌云遮青天，
东眼被遮住；
黑土埋金子，
东心被埋住。

东主骂老鹰，
不许来吃米。
老鹰吸凉风，
原因在这里。

东主骂狗獾，
不许来喝水。
狗用舌舔水，
原因在这里。

Chapter 7 The Meddling Crow
第七章 乌鸦挑唆

As the poisonous barb has hooks,
As the bad dog attacks for no reason,
When Dongzhu came by,
The crow came to stir up trouble:

"The hawk does not work on the canal,
Only chasing the fire and smoke;
The dog does not dig the dirt,
Only running after the meat.

"Day in day out on the soil,
Only I toil and moil.
Covered with too much mud to clean up,
I am always bending over like a bow."

Like the blue sky covered by dark clouds,
Dongzhu's eyes were blinded;
Like the gold buried by dark soil,
Dongzhu's heart was bewitched.

Donghzu rebuked the hawk,
Barring it from eating grains.
Hawks today breathe so much cold air,
And it all started here.

Donghzu scolded the dog,
Banning it from drinking water.
Dogs today lick water,
And it all began here.

金蜂不服气,
银蝶抱不平。
跑到东身边,
争先诉真情:

"鹰在展劲扒,
狗在埋头挖。
乌鸦乱诬告,
偷懒正是它。"

沙沉水变清,
东主怒气升。
挥起金拐杖,
砸向乌鸦嘴。

乌鸦吓一跳,
急忙躲一旁。
拍拍黑翅膀,
仓皇逃西方。

猫儿要偷鱼,
打死改不了;
乌鸦要饶舌,
百年变不了。

逃到术家来,
摆出可怜相。
翻动两面舌,
又把是非搬:

Chapter 7 The Meddling Crow

The golden bee would not stand by,
and the silver butterfly would not take it.
They went to Dongzhu
To tell him what really happened:

"It was the hawk who pushed hard
And it was the dog who dug hard.
The crow was telling the lie.
And it was the crow who didn't work hard."

The mud sank and the waters cleared,
And Dongzhu's temper was rising.
Swinging his gold mace,
He smacked the crow on its mouth.

Startled, the crow
Hurriedly dodged the attack.
Fluttering its black wings,
It took flight to the west.

Cats will steal fish,
Something that won't change by anything.
Crows will gossip,
Something that won't change at any time.

Escaping to the Shu household,
He pretended to be the victim.
The double-tongued liar
Cooked up a story again.

"你家好米委,
被东杀死了,
当作死老鼠,
埋进地狱了。

"土上开水渠,
土上撒麸糠。①
难道不气愤?
难道不悲伤?

"东叫我开沟,
泥巴沾满脚;
一天挖到晚,
累得气要脱。

"不给我吃喝,
还要打死我。
好心的术主,
难道不怜我?

"麦子变毒草,
邻里变仇家。
有气能不出?
有仇能不报?

---

① 开渠、撒糠都是为了使灵魂无法复生。

Chapter 7 The Meddling Crow

"Your poor Miwei
Was murdered by the Dongs in cold blood;
Treated like a dead rat,
His corpse was buried in hell.

"They then built a canal over it
And spread rice husks,①
So that Miwei could never rise from the dead.
Isn't it infuriating?
Isn't it sad?

"Dongzhu ordered me to dig ditches,
And I toiled day and night,
with dirt covering my feet.
I worked too hard to breathe.

"I was given nothing to eat or drink
And was almost beaten to death.
My good Shu lord,
have pity on me!

"Wheat can turn into mold
And neighbors may become foes.
How can anger not be vented?
How can one not revenge oneself?

---

① They built a canal and spread rice husks so that Miwei could never rise from the dead.

黑白之战　The War Between Dongzhu and Shuzhu

"蚯蚓没骨头，
怎能当蚯蚓？
雀子受鹰欺，
怎能当雀子？"

"Earthworms have no spine,
So how can I be an earthworm?
Sparrows are bullied by hawks,
So how can I be a sparrow?"

第七章 乌鸦挑唆
Chapter 7　The Meddling Crow

第八章　术主寻衅

母鸟失儿雏，
悲鸣鸣三天。
耿饶纳媒①啊，
痛哭哭连天。

火种借风燃，
风助火烧山。
乌鸦煽醋风，
术主捶胸膛：

"生儿生九个，
个个像猛虎，
不如米委勇，
米委是黑龙。

"生女生九个，
个个像凤凰，
不如米委好，
米委是只鸾。

---

① 耿饶纳媒：米委的母亲。

Chapter 8   Shuzhu's Provocation

Losing a young,
A mourning dove would coo for three days.
Gengrao Namo①
Cried for days.

Kindling turns into flames with wind,
Which spreads the burning to the whole mountain.
The crow fanned the wind of the inciting words
Till Shuzhu was beating his breast mad:

"All my nine sons
Are as fierce as tigers.
But none is as brave as Miwei,
who was a black dragon.

"All my nine daughters
Are as fine as peacocks.
But none was as good as Miwei,
who was a phoenix.

---

① Gengrao Namo: Miwei's mother.

黑白之战　The War Between Dongzhu and Shuzhu

"金鸡偷不来，
倒反赔了米；
日月偷不来，
倒反赔了命。

"像割我头发，
像摘我心肝，
像砍我右臂，
像挖我左眼。

"鸾鸟自碰网，
东也太欺人。
闷气难下咽，
拼死战一回！"

术主与纳嫫，
深夜在密谈；
术主与大将，
清早在商量。

肯子丹由来，
那日左普来，
米麻生登来，①
一起在筹商：

---

① 三人均为术将。

Chapter 8 Shuzhu's Provocation

"Go out for wool
And come home shorn.
We went for the sun and the moon
And ended up losing my son.

"I feel like having my hair cut,
My heart and liver removed,
My right arm chopped off,
And my left eye extracted.

"The phoenix met its own death,
But Dongzhu has pushed me too far.
I can never get over this
And would rather take on a deadly fight!"

Shuzhu and Namo
Planned secretly all night;
Shuzhu and his generals
Discussed all day.

Kenzi Danyou came,
So did Nari Zuopu,
And so did Mima Shengdeng.①
They came to join in the discussion:

---

① The three people are Shu's generals.

要带九千兵,
要选九百将,
报仇擒阿璐,
东族要杀光!

三山铁杉树,
砍下削长矛;
三谷藤与竹,
割来编铠甲。

长矛千千万,
锋利如铁锥;
铠甲万万千,
坚实像石墙。

铁匠来千个,
赶制铁盔帽;
火炉烧千个,
赶打长短刀。

犏牛杀千双,
牦牛杀千双,
弯角做硬弓,
皮条做剑弦。

山雕斩一万,
山鸡杀一万;
羽毛插箭尾,
造出雕翎箭。

They would send nine thousand soldiers,
Led by nine hundred selected generals,
To revenge on Alu
And to exterminate the Dong people!

Fir branches from the mountains
Were filed and sharpened to make spears;
Rattans and bamboos from the valleys
Were cut and woven to make armors.

Thousands of spears
Were as sharp as iron drills;
Tens and thousands of armors
Were as hard as stone walls.

Thousands of blacksmiths
Were busy making iron helmets;
Thousands of furnaces
Were burning to forge swords long and short.

Thousands of dzos were killed,
And thousands of yaks were butchered;
Their horns were made into heavy bows
And their hides, bowstrings.

Tens and thousands of vultures were killed
And pheasants were slain;
Their feathers were used
To make the vulture-featured arrows.

股股黑卷风，
刮过边界来，
刮倒白的树，
刮垮白的房。

支支黑羽箭，
射到东地来，
射落白的鸟，
射伤白的羊。

界石要崩了，
界水要决了，
火链击火石，
战火要烧了。

Chapter 8 Shuzhu's Provocation

Gusts of black whirlwinds
Were blown across the border,
Blowing down the white trees
And crushing the white houses.

Showers of black-feather arrows
Were shot to the east,
Shooting down the white birds,
And wounding the white goats.

The boundary stone was about to crumble;
The boundary river was about to burst its banks.
The fire chain was rubbing the fire stone,
And the flames of war were about to start.

第九章　遣兵侦察

天阴要下雨，
蚂蚁早知道；
术要来侵扰，
东主早料到。

金蜂当探兵，
身轻耳目灵。
东主派金蜂，
术地探真情。

金黄小蜜蜂，
飞到黑屋顶。
术家马蜂恶，
一齐来包围。

术主来拷问，
金蜂紧闭嘴；
术主来劝诱，
金蜂不搭理。

Chapter 9 Scouts Dispatched

That the rain is to come,
Ants know well beforehand.
That Shu was to invade,
Dongzhu foresaw long ago.

The golden bee, light and alert,
Was chosen to be the spy.
Dongzhu sent it out
To Shu's land to gather information.

The small golden bee was
Flying to land on the roof of the black house,
Where a swarm of ferocious wasps
swooped over and surrounded it.

Shuzhu tortured it,
But the golden bee kept its mouth shut;
Shuzhu cajoled it,
But the golden bee turned a deaf ear.

硬审有九遍,
软劝有七回。
金蜂生怒气,
螫了术一针。

术主下毒手,
割下蜂舌头。
金蜂飞回来,
忍哩软啷①嚷。

蜜蜂飞千里,
忍哩软啷叫,
有话说不清,
原因在这里。

鲤鱼当探兵,
身巧嘴伶俐。
东派金鲤鱼,
术地探实情。

金黄小鲤鱼,
游到黑屋底。
术家黑鱼狂,
群起来包围。

术主来拷问,
金鱼紧闭嘴。
术主来劝诱,
金鱼不搭理。

---

① 忍哩软啷:象声词,此处形容飞动中的金蜂发出的天然响声。

Shuzhu tried every possible means,
Tough and soft.
Finally the golden bee flew into a rage,
And stung him.

Shuzhu did the despicable:
He cut off the bee's tongue.
When the golden bee flew back,
It could only hum and buzz.

The bee could fly thousands of miles
But can only buzz
And not speak clearly:
The reason lies here.

The carp, articulate and nimble,
Was chosen to be the spy.
Dongzhu sent it out
To Shu's land to gather information.

The small golden carp
Dived to the bottom of the black house,
When a shoal of savage black fish
Rushed over and encircled it.

Shuzhu tortured the gold fish,
But it did not respond.
Shuzhu seduced the golden fish,
But it ignored him.

黑白之战　The War Between Dongzhu and Shuzhu

恶审有九遍，
甜劝有七回。
金鱼生忿心，
咬了术一嘴。

术主下毒手，
割掉鱼舌头。
金鱼转回程，
伸嘴又缩嘴。

金鱼游水里，
嘴巴缩又伸，
有话说不成，
原因在这里。

东主看在眼，
猫爪抓心坎。
又把白云派，
又将白风遣。

白风空中刮，
白云天上飘。
术地藏杀机，
一眼看透了。

白云飞下天，
向东来递信；
白风旋下天，
找东来报信：

Chapter 9 Scouts Dispatched

Shuzhu tried every possible means,
Tough and soft.
Finally in a rage,
The carp bit him.

Shuzhu did the despicable:
He cut off the carp's tongue.
The gold fish on its way back,
Could but stretch and pucker its mouth.

Goldfish swimming in the water
Could stretch and pucker its mouth
But could not say anything:
The reason lies here.

Seeing this,
Dongzhu was burning with anxiety.
He sent out white cloud,
And white wind.

White wind blew in the air;
White cloud floated in the sky.
Just one glance
Gave them a pervading sense of menace.

White wind descended
To give Dongzhu the intelligence;
White cloud stopped
To give Dongzhu a report:

"术地铠甲多,
好像树叶飘;
术地刀矛多,
好像乱草草。

"铁盔像鹰群,
战马像蚂蚁,
长弓像蛇阵,
箭似蜜蜂飞。

"会飞的在飞,
会跳的在跳,
会砍的在砍,
会杀的在杀。

"罗堆古扭来,
立了三个寨;
罗霸季登来,
立了三个寨。

"六寨鬼怪兵,
昼夜在操演。
左普是箭官,
丹由是总管。

"呆兵像狐狸,
拉兵像虎狼,
毒兵像牛头,

Chapter 9 Scouts Dispatched

"There were many armors in Shu's land,
Just like fallen leaves blowing around;
There were swords and spears everywhere,
Just like wild weeds growing here and there.

"The iron helmets were like throngs of condors;
The war horses, colonies of ants;
The long bows resembled the arrays of snakes;
The arrows whizzed like the flying of bees.

"Those who could fly were flying;
Those who could jump were jumping;
Those who could cut were cutting;
Those who could kill were killing.

"Luodui Guniu had come,
And set up three camps;
Luoba Jideng had, too,
And built three more.

"The soldiers of bad elements in these camps
Were drilling day and night,
With Zuopu as their officer
And Danyou as their head.

"Dai troops were like foxes,
And La troops, wolves.
Du troops were ox-headed

仄兵像马面。

"蒙兵像水妖,
恩兵獠牙尖。①
黑云滚滚起,
天地暗无光。"

东主听了笑,
暗笑黑魔疯。
鸡蛋碰石头,
飞蛾要扑火!

九座白山上,
白兵来布冈;
七条白谷里,
白兵来设防。

东兵站高山,
好像树满山;
东将进深谷,
好像大河淌。

阿璐像斑豹,
走路风呼呼。

---

① 呆、拉、毒、仄、蒙、恩:均为术鬼之名。

Chapter 9 Scouts Dispatched

And Ze troops, horse-faced.①

"Meng troops were like water demons
And En troops had ferocious fangs.②
The dark clouds roamed
And there was darkness without any light."

Dongzhu chuckled at what they said,
Laughing at the crazed demons:
Like eggs hurled against a rock
And moths darting into the flame!

In the nine mountains
The white soldiers set up the posts;
In the seven valleys
They strengthened their defense.

Dong's soldiers stood high in the mountains
Like tall trees all over the hills;
Dong's generals marched deep into the valleys
Like a wide river rolling through the hills.

Like a leopard, Alu
Walked like the blowing wind.

---

① The ox-headed and horse-faced refer to evil spirits in animal forms.
② Dai, La, Du, Ze, Meng, En are the names of the ghosts of the Shu's land.

黑白之战　The War Between Dongzhu and Shuzhu

斑豹下山来，
黑魔像灰鼠。

阿璐是蛟龙，
站着神抖抖。
蛟龙闹海来，
黑鬼像泥鳅。

镇海大将军，
委给阿璐当，
派去白海边，
凭海设关防：

"东族不容侮，
东土不容犯。
术兵胆敢来，
牛刀斩鸡犬！"

When the leopard came down the mountain,
The dark fiend was but a rat.

Alu was a dragon,
Full of life.
When the dragon played in the sea,
the dark ghost was but a loach.

Alu was then appointed
The general guarding the sea.
He was sent to the white sea
To fortify it against any attack.

"The Dong people will never be insulted
And its land will never be affronted.
If the Shu troops dare to try,
The butcher's knives will be waiting for those chickens!"

第十章　初战白海

黑云聚白海，
沉沉像铜块。
术兵像蚂蚁，
涌向海子边。

黑气笼白海，
茫茫不见天。
术将像黑雕，
嚎着要叼羊。

长矛像乱蜂，
朝着阿璐戳。
长刀像闪电，
对着阿璐砍。

黑手像密林，
想把阿璐吞。
麻绳像花蛇，
要把阿璐捆。

Chapter 10   First Battle at the White Sea

Dark clouds gathered over the white sea,
As heavy as copper blocks.
And the Shu's soldiers were like waves of ants,
Surged towards the seashore.

With a dark mist now blanketing the sea,
The sky became invisible.
Shu's generals were like black eagles,
Roaring and ready to lift the lambs away.

Long spears were like a swarm of wasps,
All were thrusted towards Alu.
Long swords were like shafts of lightening,
All were meant to strike him.

Dark hands were like thick forests,
Threatening to entangle Alu.
Tendrils were like venomous snakes,
Waiting to coil around him.

阿璐施法术，
海头弄旋风。
风势如狂龙，
风声如雷轰。

阿璐显神威，
海尾弄海波。
波狂像怒狮，
浪大像山峰。

飞身驾风浪，
浪立千丈高。
压向术兵群，
好像雪山倒。

术兵溃下去，
像河决了堤。
逃命嫌腿短，
爹妈喊不赢。

术将败下阵，
像城塌了门。
夺路乱相踩，
头也不敢回。

丹由压阵脚，
慌忙放妖箭。
箭头像冰雹，
纷纷落海面。

Chapter 10 First Battle at the White Sea

Alu used his magic spell:
A tornado swirled up in front of the sea,
As strong as a raving dragon,
As loud as a thunderbolt.

Alu showed his prowess:
Monstrous billows brought up by the rear,
Snarling like furious lions,
As high as mountain peaks.

Alu rode on the crest of the waves,
Which were surging a thousand feet high,
Then crushing down on Shu's soldiers
As if an avalanche had struck.

Shu's soldiers were badly beaten,
like a broken dam.
They couldn't run fast enough,
Wailing and screaming.

Shu's generals were roundly defeated,
Like a collapsed city gate.
They took flight trampling on each other,
Daring not to turn their heads.

To stabilize the situation, Danyou
Hastily shot arrows of black magic.
The arrow heads were like hails
Falling onto the sea.

黑白之战　The War Between Dongzhu and Shuzhu

阿璐潜下海，
潜进九层殿。
阿璐掀大浪，
白浪高万丈。

术兵想过海，
海浪挡齐天。
术将想跨海，
有翅难飞天。

黑箭射海心，
好像鱼群游。
大浪作护盾，
难伤阿璐头。

术主干瞪眼，
自骂是蠢材。
丹由跺脚板，
像狗团团转。

低头定心想，
抬手抓抓腮。
想出一条计，
凑近术耳讲：

"捉鹰拿鸡诱，
伏虎拿兔引。
金钩钓好汉，
香饵是美人。"

Chapter 10 First Battle at the White Sea

Alu dived into the depths of the sea,
And sneaked into the nine-storied palace.
He stirred up the powerful billows,
White billows that reached the sky.

Shu's soldiers attempted to cross the sea,
But were stopped by waves sky-high.
Shu's generals tried to fly across the sea,
But their wings were of no match.

Darting at the center of the sea,
The poisonous arrows resembled schools of fish.
But shielded by his colossal waves,
Alu stood protected.

Shuzhu could do nothing,
Blaming himself terribly for his ineptitude.
Danyou stamped his feet,
Pacing restless like a dog round and round.

Danyou gathered himself together,
Scratching his head.
Then he came up with a tactic,
And said to his master secretively:

"Hawks can be enticed with chicken,
And tigers can be lured with hare.
The golden hook for good men
Can be the bait of beauty."

风吹愁云散,
疙瘩顿解开。
术脸浮笑影,
术眼焕光彩。

Chapter 10 First Battle at the White Sea

Like winds breaking the clouds of worries,
The knots dissolved.
A smile emerged on Shuzhu's face,
And a light, in his eyes.

第十一章　耿饶茨嫫

雪山长草乌，
也会开鲜花。
阴坡刺荨麻，
也会抽琼芽。

术主和纳嫫①，
有女像朵花。
养育十八春，
长成像朵霞。

耿饶茨嫫啊，
美姿世上稀。
手似嫩竹笋，
腰似马蜂细。

纳嫫生九女，
茨嫫是心肝。
术主爱女儿，
明珠托在掌。

---

① 纳嫫：术主之妻。

Chapter 11　Gengrao Cimo

On the snowy mountains grew
Fresh flowers as well as poisonous weeds.
On the shady slopes appeared
Not only thorny nettles but jade green buds.

Shuzhu and Namo①
Had a flower-like daughter.
By the time she was eighteen,
She was beautiful as a rosy cloud.

Gengrao Cimo was her name.
Her beauty had no equal,
With fingers fine like the bamboo shoots,
And a waist small like the wasp's.

To her mother,
Cimo was the best of the nine.
To her father,
She was a pearl in the palm.

---

① Namo: Shuzhu's wife.

一觉睡得足,
三顿吃得饱。
山水任她游,
金银任她花。

术要钓鳌鱼,
拿她当饵子。
术要猎猛虎,
将她当兔子。

银针缝金裙,
金剪裁银衣。
穿得像仙女,
扮得像妖精。

头发梳成辫,
发亮像玛瑙。
宝衣披在身,
飘动像彩霞。

听母夸奖话,
茨嬷喜心头。
听术悄悄话,
茨嬷心中愁。

喜是会东子,
英名早传闻。
美人会好汉,
平生遂了心。

Chapter 11 Gengrao Cimo

Splendid feasts,
Thrilling trips,
And priceless treasures
Were all at her disposal.

When Shuzhu went fishing,
She would be the fishing bait.
When Shuzhu went hunting,
She could be the poor hare.

With glamorous clothes,
Gold and silver,
She was dressed
Like a fairy.

Her braided hair
Glittering as agates,
Her long cloak
Floating in the wind like rosy clouds.

Her mother's favorable remarks
Encouraged Cimo.
Her father's private plans
Dismayed Cimo.

The eastern prince's name
Spread far and wide.
Whoever could marry him
Would be completely satisfied.

黑白之战　The War Between Dongzhu and Shuzhu

愁是会仇人，
不是会情人。
吉凶难预卜，
不知谁伏谁？

树木能生杈，
舌头难分枝。
只有一面脸，
难做两面人。

泥巴捏神尊，
随着匠手捏。
茨媒像泥神，
任凭父母捏。

父旨不容悖，
母意难相违。
不去不甘心，
要去又惊心。

半愁夹半喜，
半假藏半真。
架起黑云彩，
急朝白海飞。

狐狸会骗人，
茨媒要迷人。
刺藤会缠树，
茨媒要缠人。

Chapter 11 Gengrao Cimo

But it wouldn't be a date with her lover,
It was a duel against her family's foe.
Who would win,
No one could know.

Trees grew branches,
But the tongue didn't fork.
She decided to play it straight,
Not knowing how to be two-faced.

In craftsmen's hands,
Clay would turn into statues.
In her parents' hands,
Cimo was the clay.

She couldn't go against
Her parents' will.
To go, she was afraid.
Not to go, she was dissatisfied.

With mixed feelings,
She started off immediately,
Leaping up to a dark cloud,
Heading for the white sea.

Like a deceptive fox,
Cimo knew how to charm others.
As the spiral vines,
She was hard to get rid of.

黑白之战 The War Between Dongzhu and Shuzhu

阿璐站海滨，
术兵逃无影。
风吹黑云降，
美人笑盈盈。

脸颊红润润，
好像堆胭脂。
牙齿白生生，
颗颗像糯米。

眼珠溜溜转，
流星滚天边。
衣摆随风荡，
一路喷喷香。

阿璐看呆了，
魂儿掉下井。
阿璐头晕了，
天地难分清。

呆了又吃惊，
晕了又清爽：
虎会学人话，
蛇会耍花招。

莫非是术主，
派来美妖姬？
莫非是魔精，
有意来勾人？

When she saw Alu standing by the sea,
Where the wind puffed the dark clouds away,
Where not the least trace of Shu troops could be found,
She beamed with delight.

She blushed a little,
As if she had just applied some rouge.
She parted her lips a little,
Showing her teeth as white as polished rice.

Her eyes balls rolled,
And the bright stars rolled to the edges of the sky.
Her clothes swayed in the wind,
And a scent of flowers wafted by.

Alu watched her,
Enchanted.
He felt dizzy,
Totally enamored.

Gradually,
He came to his senses,
Realizing
It was a trap.

Could she be from the west,
A beauty but a devil,
Sent by Shuzhu,
Bent to seduce people?

黑白之战　The War Between Dongzhu and Shuzhu

阿璐低着头，
与她不通名。
像只小水獭，
潜进碧水底。

茨嫫像饿鹰，
来回绕海飞。
轻呼柔声唤，
声声直揪心。

阿璐在海底，
偷看茨嫫影。
半天不眨眼，
半晌不呼吸。

绸衣衬缎袄，
如花衬绿叶。
绫袖配锦带，
如云烘明月。

彩丝栓发辫，
珍珠串头上。
金花插鬓边，
银蝶飞耳畔。

耳环坠腮根，
项圈吊胸前。
玉镯套手腕，
戒指闪宝光。

Chapter 11 Gengrao Cimo

Alu said nothing,
Without lifting up his head.
Then he dived into the water,
As swiftly as an otter.

Cimo flew up as an eagle in hunger,
Soaring around the waters,
With her tender calling.
Her soft voice, heartrending.

Hidden under the sea,
Alu fixed his gaze on her at a distance,
Holding his breath,
Without a single blink.

Her dress was made of exquisite silk and satin,
With harmonious patterns in red and green.
The delicate brocade matched with the silk gauze,
Was like the moon in the clouds.

Colorful ribbons were fastened to her braids,
Pearls were strung on her head,
Gold flowers were decorated at her temples,
And silver butterflies flew by her earlobes.

The earrings hung by her cheeks,
The necklace resting on her breast,
And the jade bracelets and sparkling rings,
All livened her up.

珍宝照海水，
海水亮起来。
阿璐心儿呀，
跟着亮起来。

罗裙飘海水，
海波摇起来。
阿璐心儿呀，
跟着摇起来。

Her treasures lit up the whole sea,
And Alu's heart as well.
Her dress stirred up ripples,
Both on the sea and in his heart.

第十二章　阿璐上钩

勇猛山狮子，
会被猎狗哄；
能干好男儿，
会被美人哄。

茨嫫唤千声，
海水起波纹；
茨嫫呼万声，
不闻阿璐音。

托腮想三回，
下海来梳洗。
披开墨玉发，
露出嫩脖颈。

伸出白手臂，
好像白玉梭：
穿飞在浪间，
纺丝织鲛罗。

Chapter 12   The Bait Swallowed

Valiant mountain lions,
Could be trapped by a hound.
Heroic men,
Could be tricked by a beauty.

Numerous calls from Cimo
Rippled the surface of the sea.
Numerous calls, however,
Had not got from Alu an answer.

Chin in her hands, she was lost in thought.
She then went to the sea for a bath.
Her dark hair was parted,
And the white curve of her neck was shown.

Her delicate arms stretched out,
Dancing among the waves,
Like white jade shuttles,
Flying back and forth on the loom.

黑白之战
The War Between Dongzhu and Shuzhu

一对白奶子，
好像白蝴蝶：
停在浪花间，
轻轻颤翅膀。

边洗边歌唱，
歌声多委婉。
好像五色珠，
滚落在玉盘。

"天仙世无双，
来配英雄汉；
白鹤会青松，
来会好儿男。

"术兵早走尽，
好汉快出来；
银石配金水，
来陪天女玩！"

阿璐变白鹰，
飞上白云端；
茨嫫变黑鹰，
追进白云间。

云丝悠悠绕，
云鹰双双飞；
情绵似云海，
缠绵在一起。

Chapter 12 The Bait Swallowed

Her pair of breasts were seen,
Like a white butterfly
Flapping its wings
Poised between the waves.

She sang while bathing,
With a voice so soft and sweet,
Like colorful pearls
Dropping and rolling in a jade plate:

"Like a white crane flying
To meet the green pines,
A fairy descended from the sky
To match the hero on earth.

"Since the enemies have gone away,
My hero, please soon come out.
Silver rock to match golden water,
Please come to accompany me!"

Alu transformed into a white eagle,
Soaring towards the tips of the clouds.
Cimo became a black eagle,
Chasing him after.

They flew together to their hearts' content
In the sea of the silky clouds.
The tender feelings they both had
Were as long and lingering as silk threads made of clouds.

黑白之战
The War Between Dongzhu and Shuzhu

白鹰目光锐,
瞧见黑影子;
只怕术家网,
一闪钻海底。

青蛙到蛇口,
又被吓跑了;
黑影尖声叫,
术兵退远了。

蛇身蜕蛇鳞,
变成黄鳝跑;
茨嫫脱金衣,
下海来洗澡。

开襟露胸膛,
好似开白莲;
哼起情歌调,
金嗓脆脆甜:

"一颗明星呀,
从天降下来。
落在白海边,
可惜没人踩。

"一朵鲜花呀,
云中飘下来。
谁有好福气,
鲜花落在怀。

Chapter 12 The Bait Swallowed

The white eagle had a sharp eye,
Catching a glimpse of a dark shadow.
For fear that it was his enemy's trap,
He quickly dived into the sea.

It was as if a snake let a frog slip away
Which had been so close at hand.
A scream came from the shadow
Driving the Shu soldiers away.

Like a snake sloughing its skin
And turning into a running eel,
Cimo took off her dress,
And descended to bathe in the sea.

She unbuttoned, her breasts shown,
Like white lotus in full bloom,
Humming a love song
With a voice clear and melodious:

"A bright star from the sky
Falls down to the seaside.
It is a pity that no one
Has noticed it.

"A fresh flower
Floats down from the clouds.
He who is blessed enough
Will pick it up.

黑白之战　The War Between Dongzhu and Shuzhu

"天上有仙女，
要配俊男子；
人间有好汉，
要伴美仙子。

"好汉阿璐呀，
仙子等你来。
快来配成双，
快来缔佳缘！"

阿璐变白虎，
茨嫫变黑虎。
白虎前面行，
黑虎后面追。

翻了九架山，
不见术脚迹；
穿过七座林，
没有鬼气息。

白虎放了心，
陪着黑虎玩。
深林像蜂窝，
情人酿蜜浆。

清早玩到晚，
夜幕垂下天。
黑影惊虎心，
又到海底藏。

Chapter 12 The Bait Swallowed

"The fairy from sky
And the hero from earth,
Are suited to each other
And make a perfect couple.

"My hero,
I'm waiting here for you.
Please come.
Go with me!"

Alu turned into a white tiger,
And Cimo into a black one.
The white was running,
The black was chasing.

They crossed nine mountains,
Finding no trace of any enemy.
They passed seven woods,
Catching no smell of any devil.

The white tiger finally relaxed,
Playing with its mate at ease.
The dense forest was like a beehive,
Where this pair was busy making honey.

They played all day.
As night fell, a dark shadow came.
Frightened by the black shadow,
The white tiger wanted again to hide in the sea bottom.

107

黑白之战

The War Between Dongzhu and Shuzhu

嗅着狐毛臭,
公鸡又惊飞。
到口不得吃,
狐狸怎甘心?

茨嫫又洗澡,
头发像柳条。
赤脚戏碧波,
清喉又唱歌:

"哪有海上龙,
胆小像鲫鱼?
哪有金翅鹏,
怯懦似老鼠?

"是鱼是老鼠,
快去钻土窟;
是龙是大鹏,
快来会仙女!

"虎豹回山了,
蟒蛇归洞了。
有情来相会,
莫使我心焦。"

阿璐作变化,
变头白牦牛;
茨嫫作变化,
变头黑犏牛。

Chapter 12 The Bait Swallowed

It's like the fox's smell
Would scare the cock away.
How could the fox give up
Such wonderful prey?

Cimo came to bathe once more,
Her hair, like willow twigs swaying in the breeze,
Her feet bare, splashing around.
She cleared her throat and sang:

"What kind of sea dragon
Is as timid as a crucian?
What kind of big roc
Is as cowardly as a mouse?

"Don't be a crucian or mouse
Hiding in the mud;
Be a dragon or roc,
And come to date a fairy!

"The tiger has to come home,
And the boa has to return.
Come back to me now,
And don't make me worry."

Once again,
They changed their shapes.
This time,
Into a white yak and a black dzo.

黑白之战　The War Between Dongzhu and Shuzhu

黑牛引白牛，
相随去嬉游；
高山游三夜，
不见术兵走。

山雾当罗帐，
山梁作眠床。
情长好做梦，
美梦多香甜。

白牛陪黑牛，
黑牛偎白牛。
深谷玩三天，
不见黑魔游。

谷深似酒瓮，
溪涧似米酒。
情意似酒浓，
狂饮醉悠悠。

白天放宽心，
跟着茨嫫行。
影子摞影子，
脚跟踩脚跟。

晚上壮了胆，
陪着茨嫫玩。
耳朵擦耳朵，
巴掌抵巴掌。

Chapter 12　The Bait Swallowed

The black led the white,
Into a great mountain.
They spent three nights,
Not seeing any devil.

With the fog as their silk curtain,
And ridges, their bed.
In affectionate dreamland,
They slept, sweet and sound.

The white yak accompanied the black dzo,
To a deep ravine.
They roamed for three days,
Seeing not a dark soul.

With the valley as their wine bottle,
And mountain streams, their elixir,
In the strong liquor made of passion,
They got drunk, never wanting to wake up.

By day,
He was totally relaxed,
Following her everywhere,
Almost treading upon her heels.

By night,
he nerved himself,
To snuggle up to her,
Pressing his face against hers.

走累并肩坐，
不觉太阳落；
坐累并排躺，
不知月亮落。

When tired, they rested side by side
Without noticing the sun setting.
When tired, they lay down side by side
Without noticing the moon setting.

第十三章　陷身魔窟

金鱼上了钩，
扯绳往上拉；
大路发了岔，
抬脚踩泥沼。

茨嫫对他说：
"我俩好侣伴，
天地美姻缘，
难找第二双。

"成对金鸳鸯，
要游好水塘；
成双银蝴蝶，
要绕好花园。

"有个好地方，
绿玉盖作天，
黄金铺作地，
银子铸山川。

Chapter 13   Trapped

Once the fish had bit the hook,
Pull the fishing line;
Once the trap got very near,
The prey had to be led there.

Cimo said to him:
"We love each other so much
That in the entire world,
It couldn't find another pair like us.

"A couple of golden mandarin ducks
Need a large fine pound;
A pair of silver butterflies
Require a big nice garden.

"There is a good place,
Where the sky's made of green jade;
The earth, of gold,
And the rivers, of silver.

"银树结宝果,
银鸡唱山歌,
玉叶托金花,
金蝶绕花朵。

"石上长香草,
石下金水绕,
金狗汪汪叫,
成亲好安家。"

牛犊不知虎,
见虎会好笑;
阿璐呆一呆,
乐得眯眯笑:

"走过百条路,
趟过百条河,
这般好地方,
平生没见过。

"世间无天堂,
乐土要寻找。
说的要是真,
愿去安新家。"

"花不骗蜜蜂,
蜂不瞒鲜花。
情人不撒谎,
不信快去瞧。"

Chapter 13 Trapped

There treasures grow from the silver trees;
Cocks could sing folk songs;
Gold flowers bloom among jade leaves,
With golden butterflies hovering above.

"There sweet grass sprout on rocks;
Golden streams wind under;
And golden dogs will bark to greet us.
What a nice place for a wedding."

A calf who had never seen a tiger
Would found it funny at first sight,
Opening his eyes in amazement,
Joyfully Alu said:

"I've seen much of the world
In my life,
But this place is
Really new to me.

"There's no heaven on the earth,
So happiness needed to be sought.
If what you said is true,
I would like to go there to live with you."

"Like the bee and the flower
Who can't lie to each other,
Lovers can't have secrets between them.
If you don't believe it, go and have a look."

茨媄来拉手,
阿璐心酥麻。
一步分两步,
好像蚯蚓爬。

爬上一座山,
茨媄作法来:
绿玉铺高天,
金银铺山川。

树上银鸡唱,
花间金蝶旋,
金水绕香草,
金狗叫汪汪。

阿璐看实了,
阿璐信真了,
两步并一步,
像鹿跳着跑。

茨媄告诉他:
"前面更美好。
马鹿生银角,
山骡长金鬃。"

麻雀不知海,
见海要发憷;
阿璐像家雀,
好奇又惊愕:

Chapter 13　Trapped

Walking hand in hand,
Alu felt a quiver of excitement.
But he moved
At a snail's pace.

When they reached the mountain top,
Gengrao Cimo had already cast a spell:
The sky was made of green jade,
The landscape, gold and silver.

Silver cocks were singing on the trees,
Golden butterflies were hovering above the flowers,
Golden streams were winding around the sweet grass,
And golden dogs were barking to greet them.

Alu fell for it now,
And didn't doubt any more.
Quickening his pace,
He now skipped forward as swiftly as a deer.

Cimo told him:
"There's an even better place ahead,
Where the red deer have silver horns
And the mules have golden mane."

Like a sparrow who knew little about the sea,
Alu was stunned by the first sight of it all.
He was amazed
And filled with wonder.

黑白之战　The War Between Dongzhu and Shuzhu

"我家九代祖，
代代见识多；
我家七代宗，
万物都精通。

"这般稀奇事，
九代没见过；
这般妙光景，
七代没听过！"

再爬一座山，
茨媒又作法：
鹿角银闪闪，
山骡金鬃飘。

阿璐心花开，
停下要安家；
茨媒手一摆，
把头摇三摇：

"前边更美妙，
石头会讲话，
树木会奔跑，
那里好安家。"

阿璐心儿跳，
好奇又好笑：
"酒里可掺水？
饭里可掺沙？"

Chapter 13 Trapped

"In the long history of my family,
There have appeared so many people
Who are so knowledgeable
That nothing they don't know.

"But no one has ever heard
Of such a wonderful place,
Not to mention seeing it
With the eyes of their own!"

When they got to the top of another mountain,
Cimo had played the trick once again:
Deer had shining silver horns
And mules, gleaming golden mane.

Alu could hardly contain his joy,
Wanting to settle down right away.
Cimo shook her head
At the idea in disapproval.

"It's even more wonderful farther ahead,
Because the stones can talk
And the trees can run.
That will be the best place for us."

Alu asked curiously,
His heart thumping:
"Has water been added to the wine?
Have sands been mixed with the rice?"

"臭水不做汤,
真金不掺假,
情人心相照,
不信跑去瞧。"

茨嫫来拉他,
阿璐去拉她,
三步并一步,
双鸟飞天涯。

漩涡旋落花,
越陷越深了;
大风裹黄沙,
越裹越远了。

又翻九座山,
又跨七条谷。
石头在说话,
树木在走路。

阿璐看出神:
"这里把亲结?"
茨嫫暗暗乐:
"还要走一截。"

甑子蒸花卷,
开花在上面;
茨嫫嘴里甜,
心辣冒火烟。

Chapter 13 Trapped

"The wine is pure;
There is only the rice in the bowl.
We are true soul mates,
Believe it or not."

Cimo grabbed his hand,
And then Alu lifted her up;
They ran on together,
Hand in hand.

The fallen petals got sucked into a whirlpool
Deeper and deeper;
The yellow sands got blown off by the whirlwind
Further and further.

After crossing nine mountains and seven valleys,
They finally got where,
Stones were talking
And trees were walking.

Alu watched, fascinated:
"Let's marry here, OK?"
Cimo chuckled:
"Not yet. Go a little further."

As rolls cooked in the steamer
With nice shape above but boiling water underneath,
Cimo appeared calm,
Her heart burning inside.

黑白之战　The War Between Dongzhu and Shuzhu

躲过白的风，
避开白的云，
走到交界处，
黑白见分明。

悄悄派黑风，
暗暗派黑云，
急急见术主，
匆匆报信音。

"鳌鱼吞下钩，
有脚甩不脱；
阿璐中圈套，
有翅飞不脱。"

米利术主来，
耿饶纳嫫来，
肯子丹由来，
一起细商量。

派出火焰鬼，
浓烟罩阿璐；
放出秽气鬼，
腥秽熏阿璐。

术兵上千来，
八方困阿璐；
术将上百来，
四面围阿璐。

Chapter 13 Trapped

Far away from the white winds,
Far away from the white clouds,
Now they had reached the borderland
Between east and west.

Through the dark winds
And the dark clouds,
What was sent in a haste and in secret
To Shuzhu was a message:

"Like a fish that is already hooked,
Unable to get away without any help,
Alu has been trapped,
Impossible to fly away even with wings."

Shuzhu then
Called his wife Gengrao Namo
And General Kenzi Danyou together
For an emergency meeting.

The god of fire was sent out,
To use dense smoke to suffocate Alu;
The god of foul smell soon appeared,
With the indescribable stench.

Thousands of soldiers led
By hundreds of generals
Closed in on Alu
From all sides.

脚上钉铁镣,
手上戴铁铐。
茨嫫发苦笑,
阿璐怒火烧。

羊子进虎穴,
莫想再求饶;
人到对头家,
有仇不相饶。

要悔不及悔,
要拼不得拼。
想起爹和妈,
热泪像抛沙。

Chapter 13 Trapped

Alu fought desperately
Even with feet and hands in iron cuffs.
He glared at Cimo in fury,
Who gave a wry smile in misery.

When a lamb got in the tiger's den,
It would be naive to beg for mercy.
Once he got stuck in his enemies' place,
He could not expect any mercy.

It's too late to regret.
It's too late to fight.
Thinking about his poor parents,
His eyes were filled with tears.

第十四章　术兵犯境

蜂窝失蜂王，
蜂群会乱飞；
白海失守将，
东兵不成军。

牧场无牧人，
羊群会乱跑；
东兵失统帅，
打仗乱如麻。

海里无蛟龙，
浪平好行船；
丹由驱术兵，
轻易渡海来。

山中无老虎，
有柴随意砍；
术兵闯东境，
凶狠像虎狼。

Chapter 14 Shu's Invasion

With the queen bee missing,
The beehive would be in utter chaos;
With their general lost,
The Dong troops were utterly routed.

Without the shepherd,
The sheep would run about;
Without the commander,
The soldiers were knocked out.

With the dragon gone,
The sea would be calm;
To Danyou and his men,
The sailing was so easily done.

Like the woodcutter who would fear nothing
In the mountain without a tiger,
The Shu soldiers launched a frenzied attack,
Once they got across the border.

黑白之战　The War Between Dongzhu and Shuzhu

白天东在家,
眼皮跳三跳;
晚上东上床,
噩梦绕三绕。

梦见火烧房,
梦见水冲田,
梦见蛇吞蛙,
梦见狼叼羊。

黑云阵阵滚,
涌向白云天;
黑风声声啸,
扑进白林间。

探子来报警,
守将来告急:
"阿璐失踪了,
术兵杀来了!"

东主传令符,
吹起海螺号,
擂响牛皮鼓,
忙把兵马调。

火来才舀水,
有水舀晚了;
水来才筑堤,
有堤难保了。

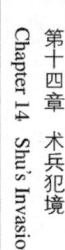

第十四章 术兵犯境
Chapter 14 Shu's Invasion

Dongzhu had three twitches
In his eyes in the daytime;
And he had recurrent nightmares
In bed at night.

He dreamed of the houses on fire,
Of the fields flooded,
Of the frogs swallowed by the snakes,
And of the sheep in wolves' mouths.

Huge dark clouds rolled up
Towards the bright sky,
Accompanied by the black winds,
Howling through the white woods.

The scouts scurried back in panic,
Shrieking, "Alu... Alu is in sight nowhere!"
The defeated generals stumbled back,
Screaming, "Enemies... enemies are everywhere!"

Hardly had their voice faded away,
The orders were given right away:
"Having the horns blown,
Drums beaten and forces deployed!"

It's too late to fetch the water
When the fire had already started.
It's too hard to dam the river
When the field had already been flooded.

黑白之战
The War Between Dongzhu and Shuzhu

垭口战三场,
乱麻绞成团。
黑剑碰白剑,
满山爆火光。

坡头战三场,
草坡秃脊梁。
黑箭撞白箭,
遍坡雷声喧。

路上战三天,
尘土飞满天。
刀口成锯齿,
盔甲变破筛。

寨前战三天,
浓烟像雾海。
汗水流满井,
血水淌成江。

垭口守不住。
山坡守不住;
路上斗不赢,
寨前斗不赢。

有将阵亡了,
有兵战死了,
不得不退了,
不得不撤了。

Chapter 14 Shu's Invasion

The narrow mountain pass
Was in a total mess,
Flashing with swords and knives,
Blasting with deafening whoops.

The grassy slopes of the valley,
Now became barren from the continuous fights,
With arrows raining down, white and black,
Whizzing past like thunderbolts.

The roads during the war about three days,
Were filled with dust clouds reaching to the sky,
With the sharp blades now growing rough saw teeth,
Helmets and armors turning into sieves.

The front of the village gate during the war for three days
Was filled with dense smoke and fumes,
Sweat streaming down all over,
And blood flowing like a river.

The mountain pass fell,
The valley was gone.
Utterly defeated,
They could also soon lose their homes.

So many generals were killed,
And so many soldiers were dead.
They couldn't fight anymore.
It's high time to withdraw.

米利东主呀,
父亲是天族。
他要躲战祸,
暂且去天宫。

色爪苟嫫呀,
是东小女儿,
跑到白山上,
躲进深谷里。

依古根库呀,
是东小儿子,
跑到白峰头,
躲进岩缝里。

五谷搬上山,
六畜吆上山。
珍珠埋岩间,
宝石埋岩间。

金嫫是龙族,
儿舅在海宫。
战火她不怕,
不愿去龙宫:

"坏事有百样,
我没做一件。
做事不亏心,
半夜心不惊。

Chapter 14 Shu's Invasion

Having a highborn father
Belonging to the Clan of Heaven,
Milidongzhu sought shelter
Temporarily in heaven.

Sezhua Goumo,
His youngest daughter,
Could not but
Hide in the deep ravine.

Yigu Genku,
His youngest son,
Had no choice but
To hide between the rocks.

Bags of grains were carried up the mountains,
And scores of livestock were driven uphill.
Pearls and jewels were all
buried and hidden under the rocks.

Jinmo, as a member of the Dragon Clan,
Had a brother reigning over the sea.
Fearless in the face of danger,
She was reluctant to escape to the sea.

"Evil deeds
I have never done.
With a clear conscience,
I've nothing to hide.

"术有千斤石,
不能压死我!
术有千把刀,
怎敢杀死我!"

黑鹰飞来了,
黑豹跑来了,
黑虎扑来了,
黑牛撞来了。

丹由射黑箭,
左普挥大刀,
季登①举利斧,
斥补②舞尖矛。

嚎着要捉东,
东走不留针;
想擒东儿女,
汗毛无一根。

黑绳捆金嫫,
术主审金嫫;
"东主去哪里?
珠宝藏哪里?"

---

① 季登:术将罗霸季登。
② 斥补:术将哈拉斥补。

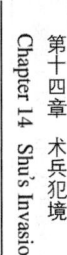

"Shu's huge rocks
Could not crush me!
Shu's thousand knives
Would not kill me!"

Black hawks dashed towards her,
Black bears sprang on her,
Black tigers pounced on her,
And black bulls charged at her.

Danyou drew a black bow,
Zuopu waved a heavy broadsword,
Jideng① swayed a sharp battle axe,
And Chibu②, a flashing spear.

They were howling wanting to catch Dongzhu,
Only to find that he was long gone with nothing left;
They were shouting attempting to find his children,
Only to find that they had vanished into the thin air.

Shuzhu then had Jinmo tied up
With black ropes and cross-examined her:
"Where is Dongzhu?
Where are the treasures?"

---

① Jideng: Shu's general Luoba Jideng.
② Chibu: Shu's general Hala Chibu.

黑白之战　The War Between Dongzhu and Shuzhu

指着白山问，
一问九摇头；
指着白海问，
九问不点头。

黑鞭像雨雪，
纷纷落满头；
翠竹不折腰，
金嫫不低头！

术兵乱砍杀：
老的站着杀，
小的睡着杀，
壮的追着杀。

烧房捉牛羊，
成群往回赶；
砸柜搜金银，
成箩往回抬。

白房白院里，
黑气冲上来；
白田白地上，
黑幕盖下来。

When asked about the white mountains,
She shook her head;
When questioned about the white sea,
She would not nod her head.

When a rain of whips
fell on her head,
She straightened herself up,
Never bowing her head.

Then Shu's soldiers launched a genocide:
The old were attacked without warning,
The young were smothered in their sleep,
And the strong were chased and then killed.

Houses were burned,
Cupboards were crushed,
Livestock were caught,
And treasures were sought.

Soon the white houses
Were enveloped in the dark smokes;
Soon the white fields
Were shrouded in the black fog.

第十五章　宁死不屈

术兵押阿璐，
趟过九条河，
穿过九个坝，
爬过九座坡。

尼青肯乌寨，
是术大本营。
阿璐押过来，
关在铁屋里。

墙上安铜刺，
墙根插铁针。
纳补乌吕①啊，
守住铁房门。

黑羊守城上，
黑鱼守城下，
獠牙瘦黑狗，
守在城半腰。

---

① 纳补乌吕：男看守名。

Chapter 15　Death over Betrayal

Escorted by the guards,
Alu waded through nine rivers,
Crossed over nine dams,
And climbed over nine hills.

Finally he reached
The Niqing Kenwu Village,
Where Shuzhu lived,
And was locked up in an iron house.

Copper thorns were all over the walls,
And iron needles protruded from the corners.
Nabu Wulv, the jailor,
Guarded the iron door.

The black goats patrolled up on the city wall,
The black fish defended the deep moats below,
And the black dogs with ferocious fangs
Guarded in the middle.

黑白之战　The War Between Dongzhu and Shuzhu

术要报儿仇，
扯弓嗡嗡响；
术要杀阿璐，
磨刀霍霍响。

东天有日月，
术想夺过来；
东地有光明，
术想抢过来。

术要东天黑，
术要东地暗；
术要术天明，
术要术地亮。

摘取日和月，
秘诀要通晓。
术主没料到，
术主不知晓。

松开射人弓，
收起砍头刀。
嫁女嫁对头，
枕边套秘法。

茨嫫钦好汉，
真情有三分；
好汉是仇敌，
真情难相倾。

Chapter 15 Death over Betrayal

The time had at last come
To kill Alu to avenge his son.
Shuzhu fitted an arrow to the string,
And sharpened his knife.

However, he hesitated upon reflection.
It was the sun and the moon
That shed lights on all,
And that he was bent on snatching.

Shuzhu wanted to make the east sky dark
And the east land dark;
Shuzhu wanted to make the west sky bright
And the west land bright.

But a password was needed
To get the sun and the moon.
It was out of his expectation.
He hadn't known this before.

He had the grips on the bows relaxed
And the knives put back in the sheaths.
He then ordered his daughter to marry Alu
In order to tease out the secret from him.

It was a mixed blessing to Cimo,
Who loved Alu as usual.
But she had to hide her true feelings,
Since they were supposed to be mortal enemies.

父旨嫁阿璐，
真喜有七分；
吉凶难卜知，
惊怕有三分。

竹篾编篮子，
凭着竹匠编；
茨媄像篾条，
只好凭父编。

家狗怕主人，
不敢不听话；
囡像乖乖狗，
只好听妈话。

真情夹虚情，
茨媄来温存。
开镣当新婿，
阿璐难解谜：

"昨日阶下囚，
何因成上宾？
莫非茨媄她，
果是抱真心？"

不辨假与真，
和美做夫妻。
水滴融乳汁，
相融在梦里。

Chapter 15 Death over Betrayal

Father's order for her to marry Alu
Filled her with much joy,
Although she knew
The future was uncertain and could be dicey.

Like the bamboo strips
That were bent by a master for a basket,
Cimo was at the mercy of her father,
having no freedom in the least.

Like a loyal dog
Unwilling to displease its master,
Cimo was a good daughter,
Unwilling to disobey her mother.

Half in joy and half pretension,
Cimo showed her affections.
Now married with shackles unbolted,
Alu was dumfounded:

"Why did she send me to jail yesterday
But treat me with such tenderness today?
Is it possible
That her love has always been real?"

Whatever the cause,
They became husband and wife.
As water and milk mixed together,
They cuddled in their sweet dreams.

茨媆好话儿，
像根糖绳子，
要捆阿璐心，
要把秘诀引：

"你是我的心，
你是我的肝；
我有心肝话，
你来听我讲。

"父亲好心肠，
金山要给你；
母亲好脾气，
银海要送你。

"说出口诀来，
讲出秘语来，
抱住金银山，
万年享不完！"

跌过一回井，
再来就小心；
落过一次网，
再来就警惕。

日月连着心，
故乡连着肝，
心肝不能丢，
秘诀不能讲。

Chapter 15 Death over Betrayal

Her words were as sweet
As honey to the bee,
Trying to tempt Alu
To give her the password:

"My sweetheart,
My honey, and my love,
I have some words from my heart.
Please listen to me.

"My dear father will give
The gold mountains to you;
My dear mother will leave
The silver seas to you.

"If you tell me the secret,
If you give me the password,
Your great wealth
Will be inexhaustible."

Like a child who burnt once
Dreads the fire,
Alu, having been trapped once,
Was on guard this time.

The sun and the moon,
A vital part of his homeland,
Were so precious to him
That he could not tell.

"岩头金马鹿,
看见灵芝草,
跑去嚼灵芝,
哪知是毒草。

"一次被蛇咬,
再次见蛇怕。
秘诀我不说,
你莫耍花招。"

茨媆劝阿璐,
九次劝不回;
茨媆哄阿璐,
九法哄不成。

再劝口干了,
再哄没话了。
茨媆刚走开,
丹由又上前:

"你是祭神羊,
拴在木桩上;
你是过年鸡,
罩在竹篮里。

"说出秘诀来,
留命在人间;
若想硬碰硬,
当做死鼠埋!"

Chapter 15 Death over Betrayal

"Once a red deer,
Found the magic herb
On the mountain rock,
It ate it but it was poisonous.

"Once bitten,
Twice shy.
I won't tell.
Save your breath!"

Cimo racked her brains
To persuade and trick him.
But all sorts of efforts
Ended in nothing.

At her wit's end, Cimo
Had nothing else to say.
But as soon as she left,
Danyou came up and said:

"You are nothing but the lamb
Offered to the gods;
You are the chicken in the basket
To be killed for the new year feast.

"Tell the secret,
And I'll let you live;
Otherwise,
You'll be buried like a dead rat!"

阿璐想太阳,
阿璐念月亮。
想东青青草,
念东肥牛羊。

"东地有甘泉,
千股万股淌;
东地有日月,
千年万年亮。

"宁可饮毒水,
宁可一人死,
不让甘泉枯,
不让光明毁!"

阿璐泪流尽,
心似石头坚。
火烧石头炸,
心儿炸不开。

阿璐绝饮食,
身似栗木坚。
木头会晒裂,
身子晒不干。

丹由来威吓,
七十七次逼;
阿璐心儿硬,
七十七次顶:

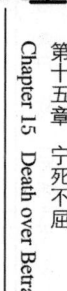

Chapter 15 Death over Betrayal

Alu missed the sun
And the moon;
He missed the eastern green grass,
Its cattle and sheep:

"Our eastern land is
Full of sweet springs.
With the sun and the moon
It is bright forever.

"Rather take the poison,
Than let the springs dry up.
Rather die alone,
Than destroy the light!"

With tears dried up, Alu had
A heart now as strong as a rock,
Which would not break
Even in flames of fires.

No longer taking food, he had
A body still stronger than a log.
A log could crack in the sun,
But his body would not.

Danyou made all sorts of threats,
Putting him through all kinds of torture.
Alu with a strong will,
Resisted in no fear.

"快来杀我吧,
东族不怕死!
术要摘日月,
除非狗变鸡!"

"Come to kill me.
We Dong people are not afraid!
But Shu could only get the sun and the moon
When the dog could turn into the cock!"

第十六章　茨嫫忏悔

术主假嫁女，
娃娃真的生：
罗池是哥哥，
罗沙是弟弟。①

三年又三月，
阿璐关屋里；
罗沙和罗池，
屋边来游戏。

罗池问看守：
"屋里关哪个？"
乌吕笑呵呵：
"是你老祖宗。"

罗沙问母亲：
"黑屋关的谁？"
茨嫫笑且悲：
"是你真父亲。"

---

① 罗池：全名哈补罗池。罗沙：全名哈补罗沙。

Chapter 16 Cimo's Confession

The fake marriage
Resulted in two sons:
Luochi was the elder one,
And Luosha was the younger.①

For three months and three years,
Alu was held captive in the house,
While Luosha and Luochi
Often came nearby to play there.

Luochi once asked the guard Wulv:
"Who was jailed in the house?"
Wulv said, smiling:
"Your old ancestor!"

Luosha asked his mother:
"Who was imprisoned in the dark room there?"
Cimo answered with a sad smile:
"It's your real father."

---

① Luochi: The full name is Habu Luochi. Luosha: The full name is Habu Luosha.

听儿问话声，
阿璐细思忖。
给儿唱个歌，
让儿去报信：

"夜空星星呀，
是天好儿孙；
我的孩子呀，
是东后代孙。

"铮铮硬骨头，
东族给了你；
圣洁血与肉，
东族塑成你。

"东地有太阳，
东地有月亮，
遍野长青草，
满山跑牛羊。

"参天百年树，
落叶要归根；
东族好子孙，
快回东家里！"

乌吕听见了，
急忙撵孩子；
乌吕害怕了，
慌忙告主子：

Hearing his sons' questioning,
Alu thought of an idea.
He could sing his sons a song,
To send a message when they sang along:

"The twinkling stars at night
Are the offspring of the sky;
My dear little children,
You're the offspring of the Dong People.

"Your powerful frame,
Your pure soul,
And your sacred blood,
Are shaped by the Dong People.

"In the east, the Dong people's world,
There are the sun and the moon,
The long green grass all over the plains,
And flocks of sheep and herds of cattle all across the mountains.

"No matter how old and big a tree is,
Its leaves fall and return to the roots;
No matter where you are, my kids,
You have to return to the east!"

As soon as Wulv heard it,
He shooed the children away;
And in great fear,
He hurried to tell his master:

"家畜和野兽,
吃草不同窝;
主人和冤家,
喝茶不同桌。

"阿璐像核桃,
咬他反断牙。
秘诀死不说,
茨嫫白嫁他。

"白天怕他唱,
夜晚怕他逃。
不如杀了他,
免得把心焦。"

术主点点头,
喊来刀斧手。
阿璐被捆绑,
押去黑海边。

左普来砍头,
毒兵来提头,
黑蚁来喝血,
黑蝶来吮油。

凶信如冰风,
刮得茨嫫抖。
嫁时像儿戏,
死别情难舍:

Chapter 16　Cimo's Confession

"Animals, domestic and wild,
Graze the same grass but live not in the same place;
My lord and your nemeses, drink the same tea
But please do not be at the same table.

"Alu is like a hard nut:
If you bite it, your teeth may get broken.
He would rather die than reveal the secret,
So Cimo's marriage to him is in vain.

"I have to forbid him from singing by day,
And prevent him from escaping at night.
It is not worth keeping him,
So better kill him for the peace of mind."

Shuzhu nodded his head.
Then Alu was soon tightly bound
And escorted by some headsmen
To the beach of the black sea.

Zuopu chopped off his head,
And Shu's soldiers took it away from his body.
The black ants came to drink up his blood,
And the black butterflies came to eat up his flesh.

The bad news chilled Cimo like the icy winds.
She trembled all over with racking sobs.
Though the marriage was like a game,
Parting made her suffer:

159

黑白之战　The War Between Dongzhu and Shuzhu

"把我嫁阿璐,
为何杀阿璐?
要儿变遗孀?
要我当寡妇?

"骗他是茨媒,
骗我是父母;
相骗到头来,
噩梦做一场!"

茨媒到海滨,
含泪瞟亲人。
面对刽子手,
忏悔放悲声:

"我爱阿璐脸,
美似日月圆;
我慕阿璐能,
巧工能开天。

"曾是真对头,
曾是假夫妻;
对头会变亲,
假也会变真。

"生儿同养育,
哪能不生情?
魔心也是肉,
哪能不动心?

Chapter 16 Cimo's Confession

"Why did you marry me to Alu,
And then kill him?
Why did you make your own child a widow
And my children fatherless?

"To him, I am a deceiver;
To my parents, I'm the victim.
My life, full of lies and deception,
Is but a horrible dream!"

She stumbled to the seaside
To have the last look of her beloved.
To the headsmen,
She said in tears:

"I loved his looks
As beautiful as the sun and the moon;
I admired his talent
So gifted that he could create the world.

"We were once true enemies,
And then a fake couple;
Enemies may turn to families,
And a fake union can become a real couple.

"Wouldn't love gradually grow
As we had and cared for our children?
Wouldn't I fall in love
As I, though an imp, still have feelings?

"骗他我有计,
救他我无能。
恨只恨父亲,
恨只恨自己。

"你们既杀他,
我只求个愿:
莫使一滴血,
染污他的脸。

"生难一同生,
死要一路行。
害他我有份,
他死我来陪!"

雷声轰一轰,
电光闪一闪。
茨嫫夺剑柄。
殉情在一旁。

黑海刮黑风,
黑海翻黑波,
黑风卷黑波,
一片黑蒙蒙!

Chapter 16 Cimo's Confession

"So clever I was when I tricked him,
But so helpless I was when I wanted to save him.
Who I hate the most,
Are my father and myself.

"Now that you have killed him,
I wish for only the following:
Don't let any drop of blood
Stain his handsome face.

"Since he and I could not grow old together,
Let me accompany him in death.
I, too, am one of his killers.
We will die together!"

The thunder crashed
And the lightning flashed.
Cimo snatched a sword
And killed herself by Alu's side.

Gusts of the black wind came by
Howling over the black sea,
Raising the black waves high to the sky.
In utter darkness, there's nothing to see!

第十七章　东主返世

白光照白云,
东主天上回。
脚踩焦土地,
手摸破烂堆。

渠里流着血,
山里抛遗体。
小孩失父母,
老人丢儿孙。

荒土不生草,
干坡不淌泉。
太阳少光彩,
月亮多凄凉。

东主来回走,
心痛像刀绞。
母虎失乳子,
眼泪像雨浇。

Chapter 17 Dongzhu's Return

Dongzhu returned from heaven
Lighting up the clouds white,
To find his home a wasteland
With burnt earth and heaps of ruins.

Blood was running through the canals,
And corpses, deserted all across the mountains.
Poor little children had lost their parents,
And old people, their children and grandchildren.

It was a desolate land with no grass growing,
A dry place with no springs flowing.
A gloomy sky with a dim sun,
And a moon that looked forlorn.

Dongzhu walked back and forth restlessly,
Heartbroken.
His tears rained down his cheeks,
As a tigress who had lost its cubs.

东主上下瞧,
心窝像锤打。
羊圈遭灾殃,
豺狼不可饶!

高高一座山,
树木全烧光。
老人下山来,
歌声多哀婉:

"老羊失小羊,
不想吃草了;
羊毛被烧光,
羊要冻死了。"

上前扶老者,
热手烫冰肠:
"刀仇要刀报,
血债要血偿!"

长长一条河,
满河扬怒波。
青年聚河滩,
歌声多激昂:

"黑魔不久长,
光明要回来;
黑夜虽漫长,
星星在发光。

Chapter 17 Dongzhu's Return

He looked around,
His heart thumping.
The sheep's pen had been broken,
And the wolf needed to be punished!

Up on the high mountains,
Trees had all been burnt up.
An old man went down the mountain,
Singing a song in deep sorrow:

"When a sheep has lost its lamb,
It will stop grazing grass.
When its fleece has been burnt in fire,
It will freeze to death."

Dongzhu stretched out his encouraging hands
To help the disheartened old man:
"Let's fight fire with fire
And give them tit for tat!"

In the long river,
Roaring waves rolled and foamed.
Young people gathered on the bank
Singing a rousing chorus with great passion:

"The black devil won't live long,
And our prospects are bright.
Although the dark night is long,
The stars are giving us light.

"不敢斩魔鬼,
不算英雄汉;
杀退术家兵,
家园要重建。

"东族弟兄呀,
快来拉弓弦;
东族姐妹呀,
快来搬石块。

"飞到术天去,
救回亲人来;
冲进术地去,
夺回牛羊来!"

歌声像火塘,
术主解了冻;
歌声像蜜水,
东主解了渴。

山头竖火把,
火光招人归;
山脚吹牛角,
角声唤亲回。

金嫫逃回来,
苟嫫出山来,
根库下岩来,
兵将聚拢来。

Chapter 17 Dongzhu's Return

"How can we be heroes
Without killing the devils?
Let's turn the table on the enemy,
And rebuild our homeland.

"Come on, brothers,
Let's draw the bows;
Come on, sisters,
Let's gather the rocks.

"Shoot the arrows to the enemy's camp
To rescue our people from them;
Attack those devils with rocks
To retake from them our flocks!"

Their song was like a blazing fire,
Melted the snow in Shuzhu's heart;
And like nectar,
Quenched his thirst.

A torch was then set on the mountain top,
Its flame beckoning the Dong soldiers back.
An ox horn resounded at the mountains' foot,
Its blare calling the Dong people home.

Jinmo soon came back,
Goumo returned from the valley,
Genku ran down from the cliff,
And the soldiers and generals were all back.

死灰有了火,
枯井有了水,
焦土有了芽,
哑嗓有了声!

It's like dying embers again flaring up,
Dry wells again filled with water,
Scorched earth again full of seeds sprouting,
And a dumb man again speaking up!

第十七章 东主返世
Chapter 17 Dongzhu's Return

第十八章　祖孙相逢

战场升炊烟，
东地庆团圆。
阿璐独不归，
如刺卡心间。

东主盼儿子，
一天盼不来，
一月盼不来，
一年盼不来。

四面找过了，
上下找过了，
中间找过了，
阿璐不见了。

一天遇千人，
怎不遇阿璐？
一夜梦百人，
怎不见阿璐？

Chapter 18 Family Reunion

Wisps of smoke rose from the wasteland,
Where people gathered to celebrate the reunion.
Alu was the only one who hadn't returned,
And Dongzhu felt as if a fishbone had stuck in his throat.

He longed for his son's return.
But he waited and waited
For a day, a month and then a year.
Alu never turned up.

He searched almost everywhere,
In the sky and on earth,
From east to west,
But found no trace of Alu.

Why hadn't he seen Alu,
As so many people passed him by each day?
Why hadn't he dreamt of him,
As so many people appeared in his dream each night?

黑白之战　The War Between Dongzhu and Shuzhu

找到若倮山，
叩问山和谷。
神山不说话，
神谷默无语。

找到达吉海，
叩问宝达树。
海不应一声，
树不答一句。

泪下如冰雹，
山虎震天啸：
"我儿阿璐呀，
莫非被术杀？"

喊声化海涛，
喊声荡云霄。
罗池听见了，
罗沙听见了。

躲过黑云手，
瞒过黑风眼，
哈补两兄弟，
跑到东地来。

孙子见祖父，
呜呜哭不休。
孤儿好伤心，
草木也悲愁：

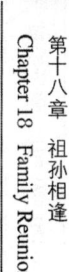

Chapter 18　Family Reunion

He flew to the celestial mountain
Ruoluo, and asked it
About Alu's whereabouts,
But the mountain was silent.

He then swam to the Daji Sea,
To ask the sacred tree
Baoda about it,
But it gave him no reply.

Dongzhu roared like a lion,
With tears coursing down his cheeks.
"Alu, my dear son,
Could it be that you were killed by Shuzhu?"

His roaring raised the storm
And stirred up the waves.
It was so loud that
Luochi and Luosha heard it.

The two Habu brothers
Came over to the east,
Having evaded the black clouds
And the black winds.

When they saw their grandfather,
They couldn't stop crying.
Seeing these orphans' sorrow,
Even the nearby plants started sighing:

"父亲阿璐啊,
被术杀死了;
母亲茨嫫呵,
跟着爹去了。"

东主哭起来,
金嫫哭起来。
龙王哭起来,
鱼虾哭起来。

东主气难忍,
眼里迸火花;
好像雷击顶,
痛得虎样跳:

"我养九个男,
没有阿璐能;
我育九个女,
没有阿璐美。

"不吃甜麦子,
吃着毒草了;
不进亲戚家,
进了仇家了。

"可悲歪天下,
躺着东族人;
可恨斜地下,
埋着能干人。

Chapter 18 Family Reunion

"Alu, our father,
Was killed by Shuzhu;
Cimo, our mother,
Killed herself afterwards."

On hearing these words, Dongzhu and Jinmo
Couldn't hold back their tears,
The Dragon King and the sea creatures
All began to cry sadly.

Dongzhu was boiling with so much rage
That he couldn't suppress it any more.
He jumped up in great pain,
Like a tiger just struck by lightning:

"Though I have nine sons,
He was the best;
Though I have nine daughters,
None could match him in appearance.

"He chose poison
Over food,
He visited his enemies
Instead of his relatives.

"In this world where
white and black were reversed,
It was the able Dong people
Who were buried in hell.

"日月般的脸,
怎能再看见?
宝石般的手,
怎能再摇晃?

"白玉般的心,
怎能再跳动?
星辰般的眼,
怎能再闪烁?"

白的天哭了,
白的地哭了,
白的风哭了,
白的云哭了。

"How I miss his lovely face,
As bright as the sun and the moon?
How I miss his warm hands,
As strong as precious stones?

"Can your heart, as pure
As the white jade, start to beat again?
Can your eyes, as bright
As the twinkling stars, begin to shine again?"

The bright sky and earth
Were weeping.
The white winds and clouds
Were crying.

第十九章　东术决战

东将来请战,
东兵来请战,
像蝶围老树,
要去围术主。

有血流快了,
有心变热了。
东主召兵将,
商量大决战。

萨利委登啊,
来当东军师;
叶世恒丁啊,
派去搬天兵。

委登变三变,
铁块落下天。
请来好铁匠,
赶做刀和剑。

Chapter 19　The Final Battle

Eastern soldiers and generals all
Offered to attend the battle,
To besiege their enemy
As butterflies surrounded a tree.

Their hot blood was boiling
And their hearts were pounding afire.
Dongzhu summoned them
To discuss the decisive affair.

Sali Weideng was appointed
The military counselor;
Yeshi Hengding was sent
To the heaven for help.

Weideng used magic
To conjure down from the sky the finest iron.
And he found the best blacksmith
To make the sharpest weapon.

打铁像雷震,
手杆像麻林;
风箱像虎吼,
火花像飞鹰。

砍下杜鹃树,
树枝削尖矛,
树皮做头盔,
树尖做刀把。

砍下铁杉树,
剖开做箭杆;
捉来白雪鸡,
做成羽翎箭。

犏牛和牦牛,
宰了千万双。
牛角做长弓,
牛皮做弓弦。

砍下岩竹来,
割下岩藤来,
剖竹做篾甲,
编藤做盾牌。

恒丁变三变,
上天请兵将。
天将似雄狮,
天马似大象。

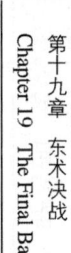

Chapter 19 The Final Battle

The sound of iron beating
Resembled thunderclaps,
Down came the hammer,
And out flew the sparks.

The azalea trees were chopped off,
Their branches sharpened to be spears,
Their skins peeled to make helmets,
And their tips cut off to serve as knife handles.

Cedar trees were cut down
To make arrow shafts;
The white snow chickens were caught
To make arrow feathers.

Thousands of dzoes were killed,
And thousands of yaks were killed.
Their horns were made into long bows,
And their hides, bowstrings.

Bamboos from the mountains
Were used as armors;
Rattans from the valleys
Were woven into shields.

Hengding flew to the heaven
To bring more reinforcements,
Led by the lion-like heavenly generals,
Riding the elephant-like heavenly horses.

黑白之战　The War Between Dongzhu and Shuzhu

优麻爱光明,①
优麻请来了;
电神恨黑暗,
电神请来了。

白风去侦探,
术地杀气荡:
八十一个寨,
屯满黑鬼怪。

白云去巡察,
术地兵如麻。
黑石砌城堡,
砌了九个堡。

金蜂去查天,
术天黑云翻。
兽怪千百个,
死守大寨前。

蝙蝠去探路,
术路脚难踩。
铜棘像竹笋,
铁铡像石滩。

---

① 优麻:护法神。

Chapter 19　The Final Battle

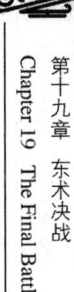

Youma, the god of protection,
Who loved brightness, was invited;
The god of lightning,
Who hated darkness, was too invited.

The white wind was dispatched ahead.
The west was a sinister place,
With eighty-one villages
Full of black monsters.

The white cloud was sent out afterwards,
Only to find many soldiers
And nine castles
With black rocks.

The golden bee went to inspect the sky,
Where the black clouds rolled up,
And monsters guarded
Everywhere in front of the village gate.

The white bat flew there as a pathfinder,
Only to find the ground too rough,
Covered with copper thorns like bamboo shoots,
And iron blades like the stony beach.

黑白之战　The War Between Dongzhu and Shuzhu

优麻磕牙齿，
天空巨雷轰；
优麻伸舌头，
天空现彩虹。

优麻竖竖尾，
高峰刮大风；
优麻翘翘胡，
魔鬼被吓懵。

优麻一怒吼，
术天发了抖。
好像面筛子，
上下抖不休。

优麻一眨眼，
术地打寒战。
好像打摆子，
摇摆又晃荡。

天上隆隆响，
地上尘土扬。
东兵追术兵，
好像赶山羊。

金头白肚狮，
咬断黑龙腰：
术主九个堡，
破了第一堡。

Chapter 19 The Final Battle

Youma ground his teeth,
And the thunder rumbled in the sky;
Youma stuck his tongue out,
And a rainbow appeared up high.

Youma lifted his tail,
And strong winds blew down the hill;
Youma got his whiskers up
And the monsters freaked out.

Youma uttered a furious roar,
Vibrating the sky over the west,
Like a shaking sieve
Without stopping.

Youma blinked his eyes,
And the whole west trembled,
Like a man, shaking all over,
Suffering from malaria.

With the claps of the thunder,
In the clouds of the dust,
The Dong soldiers chased the Shu soldiers
As if driving the goats home.

The sacred lion with the golden head and white belly
Snapped the black dragon in half.
The first castle of the nine,
Was captured.

黑白之战　The War Between Dongzhu and Shuzhu

绿壳穿山甲,
穿透黑虎腰:
术主九个堡,
破了第二堡。

孔雀张翅膀,
叼起黑蛇甩:
术主第三堡,
转眼化黑烟。

金虎大爪子,
压扁赤眼鬼:
术主第四堡,
转眼化土堆。

银头白云豹,
咬死铁头狗:
术主第五堡,
塌成一条沟。

白铁神錾子
錾倒石头门:
术主第六堡,
塌成一摊灰。

白螺雕宝弓,
射死黑甲魔:
术主第七堡,
像灶砸了锅。

Chapter 19　The Final Battle

The green pangolin pierced a hole
On the waist of the black tiger.
The second castle of the nine,
Was captured.

The peacock spread its wings,
Picked up the black snake and threw it away.
The third castle, owned by Shuzhu,
Disappeared instantly in black smokes.

The golden tiger with its giant paws
Smashed the red-eyed demon.
The fourth castle of Shu's
Became immediately a pile of ruins.

The white-cloud leopard with a silver head,
Killed the iron-headed dog with its sharp teeth.
The fifth castle of Shu's
Collapsed into a canal.

The sacred white-iron chisel
Prised open the stone gate.
The sixth castle of Shu's
Fell into a mount of dust.

The treasure bow made of the white sea shell,
Shot dead the fiend wearing a black armor.
The seventh castle of Shu's
Became a broken pot.

黑白之战
The War Between Dongzhu and Shuzhu

白铁砍天刀，
斩断黑旋风：
术主第八堡，
好像雪山崩。

锋利神铁锯，
锯死黑角牛：
术主第九堡，
像灯尽了油。

刀剑像星星，
长矛像海潮，
箭镞像下雨，
杀鬼像切瓜。

东兵和东将，
源源不断来，
狂风扫落叶，
术寨一扫光：

一将骑白虎，
斩了鹿头怪。
东兵涌上来，
破了鹿骨寨。

一将骑金象，
斩了牛头怪。
东兵涌上来，
破了牛骨寨。

The magic steel chopper
Cleaved the black whirlwind in two.
The eighth castle of Shu's
Rolled like an avalanche.

The magic iron saw
Cut up the black-horned bull.
The ninth castle of Shu's
Was like a lamp running out of oil.

Swords were sparkling like stars;
Spears were dashing like tides;
Arrows were falling down like rains;
The enemies were cut up like melons.

Dongzhu's troops came
In a steady flow.
They swept the Shu villages
Like the strong winds blew off fallen leaves.

A general riding a white tiger
Killed the deer-headed monster.
The Dong soldiers swarmed forward,
And captured the Deer Bone Village.

A general riding a golden elephant
Killed the bull-headed monster.
The Dong soldiers swarmed forward,
And captured the Bull Bone Village.

一将骑白狮,
斩了马头怪。
东兵涌上来,
破了马骨寨。

一将骑白狼,
斩了羊头怪。
东兵涌上来,
破了羊骨寨。

一将骑豹子,
斩了狗头怪。
东兵涌上来,
破了狗骨寨。

一将骑神鹏,
斩了鸡头怪。
东兵涌上来,
破了鸡骨寨。

一将骑水獭,
斩了蛙头怪。
东兵涌上来,
破了蛙骨寨。

一将骑金獐,
斩了蛇头怪。
东兵涌上来,
破了蛇骨寨。

Chapter 19　The Final Battle

A general riding a white lion
Killed the horse-headed monster.
Dong soldiers swarmed forward,
And captured the Horse Bone Village.

A general riding a white wolf
Killed the goat-headed monster.
The Dong soldiers swarmed forward,
And captured the Goat Bone Village.

A general riding a leopard
Killed the dog-headed monster.
The Dong soldiers swarmed forward,
And captured the Dog Bone Village.

A general riding a sacred bird
Killed the cock-headed monster.
The Dong soldiers swarmed forward,
And captured the Cock Bone Village.

A general riding an otter
Killed the frog-headed monster.
The Dong soldiers swarmed forward,
And captured the Frog Bone Village.

A general riding a golden river deer
Killed the snake-headed monster.
The Dong soldiers swarmed forward,
And captured the Snake Bone Village.

一将骑大鳌,
斩了鱼头怪。
东兵涌上来,
破了鱼骨寨。

放出白风云,
压住黑风云;
放出金翅鸟,
吞了黑鹊鸟。

放出白铁斧,
砍尽黑铁桩;
放出白梭镖,
凿穿术水塘。

东兵到东方,
杀九个木鬼,
斩当饶吉补,①
破了木堡垒。

东兵到南方,
杀九个火鬼,
斩时知吉补,
破了火堡垒。

---

① 当饶吉补及后面所列的时知吉补、勒钦斯普、奴朱吉补、米麻生登,分别为东、南、西、北、中五方鬼王。

A general riding a gigantic fish
Killed the fish-headed monster.
The Dong soldiers swarmed forward,
And captured the Fish Bone Village.

White winds and clouds were sent out
To prevail over the black winds and clouds.
The golden-winged birds were released
And they swallowed the black magpies.

The white steel axes were unleashed,
To level all the black posts;
The white drills were used,
To break through Shu's ponds.

The Dong soldiers went to the east
To kill the nine wooden goblins
And the king Dangrao Jibu,①
Capturing the wood fortress.

The Dong soldiers went to the south
To kill the nine fiery sprites
And the king Shizhi Jibu,
Capturing the fiery fortress.

---

① Dangrao Jibu, Shizhi Jibu, Leqin Sipu, Nuzhu Jibu and Mima Shengdeng are five ghost kings in charge of the five directions, namely, the East, the South, the West, the North and the Center.

黑白之战　The War Between Dongzhu and Shuzhu

东兵到西方,
杀九个铁鬼,
斩勒钦斯普,
破了铁堡垒。

东兵到北方,
杀九个水鬼,
斩奴朱吉补,
破了水堡垒。

东兵到中央,
杀九个土鬼,
斩米麻生登,
破了土堡垒。

金头白猿猴,
挥斧捉凶首。
术主拿住了,
纳嬷拿住了。

砍了术的兵,
宰了术的马。
丹由逃不了,
左普逃不了!

烧毁术的城,
冲毁术的地,
灭掉术的火,
截断术的水。

Chapter 19　The Final Battle

The Dong soldiers went to the west
To kill the nine metal hobgoblins
And the king Leqin Sipu,
Capturing the metal fortress.

The Dong soldiers went to the north
To kill the nine water devils
And the king Nuzhu Jibu,
Capturing the water fortress.

The Dong soldiers went to the middle
To kill the nine earthen devils
And the king Mima Shengdeng,
Capturing the earthen fortress.

The white golden-headed monkey
With an axe
Caught the rebel leaders:
Shuzhu and Namo.

Now that the Shu soldiers
And their horses were all abolished,
Neither Danyou nor Zuopu
Could escape.

Shu's towns and farmlands
Had all been destroyed;
All his fires were put out
And rivers, cut off.

敏锐黑眼睛,
挖掉不留它;
能飞黑翅膀,
削掉不留它。

会射黑手腕,
割掉不留下;
善跑黑脚杆,
砍掉不留下。

割下术主头,
雕成记功碑;
取下术主骨,
镂成号角吹。

术地翻做天,
术天割做地。
术狗不吠了,
术鸡不啼了。

宰牲祭先烈,
超荐阿璐灵;
燃柏做祈祷,
超荐茨嫫魂。

圣香驱秽气,
圣水洗妖腥。
符咒压魔鬼,
永世难翻身。

Chapter 19 The Final Battle

The sharp black eyes
Were cut out;
The capable black wings
Were plucked out.

The black hands of the bowmen
Were chopped off;
The quick black feet of infantrymen
Were cut off.

Shuzhu was beheaded,
His skull then
Carved into a memorial tablet
And his skeleton made into a horn.

Shu's land was turned into the sky
And his sky, land.
Dogs stopped barking
And cocks ceased crowing.

Sacrifices were offered
To release Alu's spirit.
Cypress trees were burnt with prayers
To expiate Cimo's spirit.

Sacred incense was burnt
To drive away the foul air,
Sacred water was applied to wash off the wicked dirt.
A spell was cast on the devils so that they would never recover.

第二十章　光明永存

黑道无人助，
白道众心归。
黑暗地底沉，
光明天上升。

用升量珠宝，
用柜装金银，
厚礼献优麻，
犒劳天神兵。

天兵回天宫，
百姓庆凯旋。
大碗喝热奶，
大盅饮酒浆。

篝火烧起来，
鼓乐奏起来，
千人舞起来，
万众唱起来：

Chapter 20 The Eternal Light

Darkness got no help;
Light enjoyed abundant support.
Darkness sank under the ground;
Light went up to the sky.

Chests of gems,
And boxes of gold
Were offered up to Youma;
And feasts, to the heavenly army.

After seeing off the heavenly soldiers,
People began their celebration:
Drinking milk with big bowls
And wine in large cups.

Bonfires were lit up;
Bells and drums were played;
Dances were danced;
Chorus was sung.

"豺狼闯羊圈,
自掘坟墓埋;
术魔逞凶狂,
自投黑罗网。

"白鹿脱虎爪,
白羊脱狼爪,
白雀脱鹰爪,
白鱼脱獭爪。

"东族得胜利,
焦山又绿遍;
光明得胜利,
千河又淌满。

"太阳更温暖,
月亮更清朗,
松柏千年翠,
泉水万年甜!"

白的天笑了,
白的地笑了,
白的风笑了,
白的云笑了。

天空平展展,
天空亮堂堂。
大鹏翩翩飞,
白鹤自在鸣。

Chapter 20　The Eternal Light

"The wolves got into the sheep's pen
To dig their own graves;
The Shu devils played havoc
To cause their own destruction.

"It is like the white deer having narrowly escaped from a tiger,
Or the white lamb from a wolf,
Or the white sparrow from an eagle,
Or the white fish from an otto.

"Since the Dong people have won,
The burnt mountains turn to green again;
Since light has triumphed,
All the rivers are filled again.

"The sun will be warmer,
The moon will be clearer,
The pines will turn green permanently,
And mountain springs will become sweet forever!"

The white sky laughed;
The white lands laughed;
The white winds laughed;
The white clouds laughed.

In the clear and
Bright sky,
A giant roc danced gracefully,
And a white crane sang freely.

黑白之战　The War Between Dongzhu and Shuzhu

大地像金毯,
六畜像金丸,
五谷像珍珠,
遍地滚起来。

高山高岩间,
百鸟唱得欢,
百兽跳得欢,
百花开得欢。

大海深湖里,
银龙戏碧水。
水下结珠贝,
水上鱼成队。

黑风不敢犯,
魔气不敢缠。
高碑刻平安,
大路皆康庄。

干戈化锦绣,
剑火化香甜。
吃的堆成山,
穿的铺成海。

少男和少女,
有了好姻缘;
老翁和老妇,
得了好寿岁。

Chapter 20 The Eternal Light

The earth was like a golden carpet,
Where domestic animals like gold balls,
And grains like pearls,
Rolled all over.

High up in the mountains,
All sorts of birds chirped merrily,
All kinds of beasts jumped happily,
And various flowers were in full bloom.

Deep down in the sea and lakes,
The silver dragons played with the water.
Pears grew with abundance under the water,
And fishes in schools swam in the water.

The black wind wouldn't dare to come,
And the evil air vanished into the thin air.
A monument was erected for peace,
And all the roads led to happiness.

Chaos gave way to prosperity,
And bitterness to sweetness,
With ample food and clothing
Piling up high to the sky.

Young men and young women
Had happy marriage;
Old men and old women
Enjoyed long and healthy life.

雪山年年白,
东族代代传;
鲜花开不败,
东族永不衰。

金线绣太阳,
银线绣月亮,
玉线绣星星,
七星①闪异彩。

太阳千秋照,
月亮千秋亮,
星星千秋明,
光明千秋在。

---

① 七星：指绣饰在纳西族妇女披肩上的七个彩色圆盘。

As the snowy mountain was white all the year round,
Dong people thrived one generation after another;
As a flower which would never wither,
Dong people would never decline.

The gold thread was used to embroider the sun,
The silver thread was for the moon,
And the jade thread for the stars,
Seven twinkling stars.①

The sun would always shine,
The moon would give permanent light,
And the stars would be bright forever,
So there was eternal light.

---

① The woolen tippet used by the Naxi women is embroidered with the sun, the moon and seven stars which are the seven colorful round patterns.